BETRAYAL IN VENICE

David Canford

COPYRIGHT © 2017 DAVID CANFORD

8.24

All rights reserved. No part of this publication may be reproduced, distributed, or transmitted in any form or by any means, or stored in a database or retrieval system, without the prior written permission of the author.

This novel is a work of fiction and a product of the author's imagination. Any resemblance to anyone living or dead (save for named historical figures) or any entity or legal person is purely coincidental and unintended.

Cover Design By: Mary Ann Dujardin

To my parents

CHAPTER 1

1971

A day he didn't want to come would soon be here.
Hot and tangled in his sheets, sleep had eluded him. He got out of bed and pulled back the curtains.
The lagoon was still black, lit only at its edges by soft lamplight coming from the promenade below. In the east, there was that first hint of dawn. The sky wasn't quite so dark, almost imperceptibly so.
Before long the sun would rise. Like curtains opening on a stage, it would reveal the vista which had so thrilled him the first time he had stayed at the Danieli all those years ago.
Centre stage would be the island of San Giorgio Maggiore, the red brick tower with its green pointed roof, the white frontage of the church with huge pillars and a triangulated top, its rounded grey dome behind. A mixture of east and west which combine to make Venice so seductive. The campanile as though a minaret and the church frontage classic Roman in style.
In the wings to the right, would be the working

class island of Giudecca, and to the left the lagoon, with backstage the Lido keeping the Adriatic at bay and the city from being submerged beneath its waters.

Front stage, gondolas tied to their moorings would be bobbing about, and small waves lapping at the pavement would create a pleasing sound of tranquility. A moment of quiet before the city woke.

Then vaporetti would begin arriving at the landing stage in front of the hotel, bringing in the workers who could no longer afford to live here, priced out by the wealthy foreigners who wanted to claim a piece of this architectural wonder for themselves. The Riva degli Schiavoni below would see the first tourists of the day heading towards Piazza San Marco, St. Mark's Square, following their tour leader like obedient schoolchildren. They would rush from monument to monument to tick them off their list, but never spending enough time to really appreciate any of them.

And so another day would begin, as it always did, at the world's greatest tourist attraction. But not for him.

This day would be like no other. His view was blurred, like an out of focus photograph. He rubbed his eyes to clear the tears forming. Soon he would know whether he had done the right thing. If she would live. And if she did, would she ever forgive him for betraying her?

CHAPTER 2

1943

It was November. He didn't know the exact date or which day of the week it was, but he did know it must be about three in the morning.

The dark waters of the lagoon were uninviting. Their hands had become numb as they paddled, wind chill reducing the temperature to below zero. Powered by adrenaline, they made no noise save for the almost undetectable sound of water being displaced by their forward strokes.

Barely visible against the night sky were the unmistakable towers and domes of la Serenissima, as though a fairytale fantasy land awaited them.

Glen Butler had long dreamed of visiting this place. He'd imagined himself walking its narrow alleyways while he absorbed its incredible history, but the reality of war had got in the way. Now his wish to visit Venice was being fulfilled in a way he had never wanted.

Thanks to his fluent Italian, Glen had been selected for this mission, if thanks were the right word. If they succeeded, he and his companions would be heroes. Success would be measured by result, regardless of whether they lived or died. If they were caught, execution for being commandos was assured. The Nazis didn't consider captives from commando raids to be covered by the normal conventions for prisoners of war.

It had been shortly before midnight when they climbed out of the conning tower and onto the top of a surfaced submarine in the northern Adriatic. They assembled their folding canoes, with sides made of canvass and a flat bottom and were ready to go. That is as ready as they ever would be. None of them really wanted to leave the cocoon of the submarine, but they had no choice. This was war, total war. King and country expected them to do their duty.

"The shore's a mile or two to the west. We'll be waiting here tomorrow after midnight. If you're not back by six in the morning, we'll have to leave and you'll need to make your way as best you can up to Switzerland or go south until you reach the front line. Good luck."

The captain and another held the back of each canoe to slow its speed as they slid off the submarine into the sea. When they were all on the water, the three canoes, each paddled by two soldiers, began their journey towards land.

From the rear of one, Glen glanced backwards. The outline of the conning tower was disappearing beneath the waves as the submarine dived. They were alone now. Whether they made it back depended on them, them and fate.

Waves lifted them from behind, sometimes turning the canoes sideways and threatening to swamp them. They struggled to keep a straight course, but after less than an hour they could make out the beach. Glen hoped it was deserted, that it wasn't patrolled at night. They were too close in now to avoid it.

A wave brought them quickly ashore and the canoes were swung at right angles to the sea. They jumped out as fast as they could before the next wave hit them, risking an almost certain capsize. They grabbed the canoes and pulled them clear of the water.

"Let's get them into the undergrowth," said Lieutenant Burridge, who was commanding the operation.

"You can take a ten minute break before we continue," he said once they were off the beach. "As we're here now, I can brief you properly."

The others sat facing him, their facial features indistinct in the darkness.

"The long and short of it is our mission is to dynamite the road bridge between Mestre and Venice. Our intelligence is Adolf Hitler will be crossing it tomorrow evening. If we succeed in killing him, it could end the war."

"Hitler," exclaimed the other five in incredulous unison.

"Fuck," added Euan Jones, exhaling the word slowly.

"I couldn't have put it better myself, Jones. It seems that the Führer wants to see the sights. Provide some good morale boosting newsreel footage no doubt. They say he felt humiliated and upstaged when he came here in thirty-four to meet Mussolini. Il Duce was dressed up like a peacock in his military uniform, projecting power and glory. Hitler arrived in his civvies, looking like the supplicant.

"Now Mussolini is his puppet, holed up in Salo on Lake Garda after the Nazis rescued him from the Italian government in September. He's a leader in name only. After the new government signed an armistice with the Allies, the Huns took over most of Italy and they make all the decisions. The man spends his days drinking and cavorting with his mistress, they say.

"This is a momentous opportunity, lads. There'll be medals galore if we succeed. But first, we need to portage the canoes to the lagoon. It's about a mile. Entering by where it joins the Adriatic would have been much too risky. We're then going to paddle across the lagoon, and lie low in the marshes until nightfall. Then we paddle to the bridge under cover of darkness, attach the dynamite and Bob's your uncle.

"Luckily, the bridges have been designed to be easily destroyed. Venice was a true island until the railway bridge was built last century, and the Venetians insisted that the bridges be constructed for easy destruction in case Venice was ever threatened. After all, it was Venice being an island which kept it safe for over a thousand years until it succumbed finally to Napoleon in the late 1700s."

"I didn't know you were the bloody Encyclopaedia Britannica, sir," said Glen.

"Not exactly, Butler. I studied Venetian history at Cambridge before the war.

"How will we know when to set the timers for?" asked Angus McPherson, a wily Scotsman.

"There are no timers. We'll be remaining nearby so that we can detonate by wire at the correct moment."

Burridge could sense the anxiety in their silence, their hopes of watching the explosion from a safe distance before making a quick escape shattered. This was no time to let them dwell on it.

"Right, let's get a move on. We don't want to be caught with our pants down come daylight. We'll be sitting ducks if we're still out in the lagoon when day breaks."

The terrain which they had to cross was flat. Pine trees gave off a pleasant aroma in the damp night air. They could make out the contours of an occasional dwelling and adjusted their course to keep well clear of them.

It wasn't long until they reached the lagoon and were able to put their canoes back in the water. Like a protective moat, it has defended Venice for centuries. Shallow for the most part, only a few feet deep at low tide, would be invaders had been kept at arms' length.

As a consequence, Venice is one of the world's few great cities not to have suffered damage from war. Genoan warships had foundered here, and the Ottoman Turks never ventured in from the open sea for fear of the same fate. In those days, the lagoon's navigable channels were a closely guarded state secret.

Tonight, the shallow draft of their canoes would be essential to enable them to make the crossing.

The blackout imposed by the Nazi occupiers meant there was almost total darkness which suited the attackers' purpose. Features, of which there were few, were just a darker shade of night.

They had to go around Sant'Erasmo, the largest island in the lagoon after Venice itself. They slipped along its eastern shore, rounding its northern end before eventually passing south of Burano. Venice now lay about five miles to their southwest. They were navigating a course well away from it, making instead for the far end of the lagoon.

A few small individual lights were visible in the distance. Locals out on their boats to harvest the pescatarian bounty of this salty larder.

Glen was suddenly jerked forward and his canoe juddered to an unexpected stop.

"We've run aground," said Angus.

They got out. Angus tried pulling and Glen pushing. Water and slime flooded over the top of their boots as they squelched along, their feet sinking into the glutinous mud. The others were walking too. Burridge called a halt.

"Maybe those wooden posts mark the deeper channels," suggested Jones.

"The bricole, yes they do. They mark the shipping channels. They'd be too dangerous for us to use. We could meet a German patrol boat. We must keep on walking until we find deeper water. I'd say we've less than three miles to go."

They tied rope to the front of the canoes. Harnessing it over the front of their shoulders, they pulled like shire horses.

While the sludge in their boots had at first felt strangely comfortable like some spa treatment, their feet were now rubbing and beginning to blister. They were tired and hungry. It had been a long night with no sleep. They didn't succeed in finding deeper water for most of the way and progress was slow.

The sky began to lighten behind them. The black blanket which had protected them began to fray with cracks of light. As dawn grew in strength, they could see that they still had a mile to go to the sanctuary of the marshes where they would spend the day waiting for night to arrive.

Fear of discovery propelled them, their exhaustion temporarily forgotten. If they were spotted out here, it wouldn't be many minutes until a fighter plane would be buzzing them and discharging its machine guns.

CHAPTER 3

As that primeval orange ball breached the horizon, they gratefully hauled the canoes into the grasslands near what is now Marco Polo airport but which then didn't exist. Like nesting birds out of sight of their predators, they would be safe here unless they were unlucky enough to be spotted from the air.

They ate some of their cold rations and fell asleep on the soggy ground. Heavy rain woke them. They passed a miserable day, unable to move around properly to get warm or dry. Lighting a fire carried too much risk of being seen.

They were reduced to crawling about. If they stood up, their upper halves would be visible. In this landscape, anything higher than the reeds was as noticeable as a flashing beacon.

During the afternoon, clouds cleared and a weak November sun provided some relief. Conversations were few, each man lost in contemplation about loved ones who he might never see again and regrets for things not said.

As the sun sank, Glen slithered forwards like a

snake, pushing reeds aside until he had a clear view. The Venetian skyline was framed by a pink tinge which was turning to crimson. Nature's brushstrokes were better than any painting.

Let me live, let me go there one day, he soundlessly pleaded. The city was the sweet shop he had stood outside of as a child, his current position the pane of glass which his nose had pressed against while he salivated at all the goodies he yearned to taste if only he'd had some money. Glen wanted to linger, etch the contours of the city onto his memory, but he could hear already his colleagues preparing to leave.

Burridge issued final instructions.

"We will detonate six consecutive arches, two each. There's likely to be more than one vehicle, and we want to make sure we get the bastard. We'll fix the dynamite to the bridges, and then withdraw a suitable distance and set off the detonators that we each have when I give the command to do so. The ensuing explosion and chaos should give us a decent chance to make our escape."

"Won't the Gerries switch on searchlights, sir?" asked Jones.

"I can't say. It's a risk we'll have to take. I'll take two arches with Smith here. I'll be farthest west, that is away from Venice itself. Jones and Dunhill, you'll take the next two, that is between where I will be and Venice and, Butler and McPherson, you'll take the two after that, that is closest to the Venice end. Is that understood?"

"Yes sir," they replied as one.

"Good. We'll move out in fifteen minutes. I suggest you all eat something beforehand. After we leave, I want absolute stillness from you chaps. No rustling around in the boats, not even to scratch your arses. Any noise could see us all ending up dead."

A couple of hours later, they glided under the arches of the railway bridge and then the road bridge next to it, creating hardly a ripple on the water. There was no indication that they might be expected. All was perfectly quiet.

With shaking hands, Glen attached a charge under his first allotted arch. He and Angus then carefully manoeuvred backwards before paddling forwards again to the adjacent arch to repeat the process. Then they withdrew, carefully winding out the wires attached to the charges until Burridge signalled at them to halt. His calculation that they were far enough away from the bridge so as not to be seen by a vehicle crossing it, seemed uncomfortably close to Glen.

Renamed Ponte della Liberta after the war finished to mark the end of fascism and the Nazi occupation, the bridge had been christened Ponte Littorio when Benito Mussolini had opened it only a decade earlier with great pomp and ceremony.

Glen could make out the shape of his comrades sitting low in their canoes. He hoped Hitler and his convoy would soon appear. The longer they sat here, the greater the risk of discovery. Occasional vehicles went past on the bridge, but Burridge gave no command.

The waiting ground at Glen's nerves like a dentist's drill. He was nauseous with fear. Why did he have to be here? I don't want to die, he told himself. I haven't lived. I'm only twenty-two. I haven't loved. I've achieved nothing. If I die, who is even going to remember me?

But war has no qualms or conscience. It takes the young without remorse. It kills without discrimination. Glen had seen enough combat on ship convoys these past few years to know that.

"Was ist das?"

A German voice rang out from the bridge. Two figures appeared, then more.

A powerful light came on turning night into day. It swept in an arc away from where they sat in their canoes. Glen held his breath, hoping. It swung back in their direction.

The sound of firing sounded unreal at first, but Angus slumping forwards in front of him was real enough.

Glen threw all his weight onto the left side. As the canoe capsized, he saw the others jolt helplessly in the beam of light while bullets peppered them.

The cold water made Glen want to surface and gasp for air but he couldn't. He would be seen and shot like the rest. His instinct to survive kicked in. Glen's initial panic subsided and he began to think what he needed to do. Cautiously raising a hand, he touched the side of the upturned canoe.

He manoeuvred himself until he was inside it and came up in the air pocket which had been created.

A sharp pain shot down his left side. His fingers moved down to touch the effected area. Glen winced and removed his hand. He too had been shot.

Knowing that he needed to get away from here if he were to have any hope of survival, he took a large breath and submerged himself in the shallow water, clawing at the slimy mud to stay fully submerged.

If he advanced, he should with any luck be moving towards the cover of the road bridge. Once under the arches, he could come up to breathe and assess what to do next.

Fighting the urge to inhale, he continued as far as he could. The pressure built inside his head until it seemed it would burst. It was no good, he had to breathe. All around him the water was dark. That must be a good sign. He surfaced.

More lights were now on the water, but on the canoes behind him. Going back under quickly in case they should shine on him, he moved ungracefully until the need for oxygen forced him up again. This time he was close to the bridge. One more descent into the water should do it.

He reached the cover of the bridge. All Glen had to do now was reach land. He stumbled forwards to the other side of an arch. He could hear nothing close by. The shouting appeared to be coming from farther away than before.

Glen crossed to the underside of the adjacent railway bridge. Staying close to the far side of that bridge, he pushed through the water towards Venice, hoping that his luck would hold. To get to Mestre and the mainland on the other end of the bridge over two miles away was simply too far, even though that offered a much greater chance of escape.

He didn't know how he would hide if he succeeded in getting to the city. Perhaps he would find a small boat he could take. At this time of night, the population should be sleeping.

Glen believed he had a fair idea of how to get to where they'd landed on the beach last night, and then he could head east out to sea to try and locate the submarine. Provided the Germans were still focused on the bridge, he might stand a chance. However, if it looked too dangerous, he could hide in the marshes, and then decide what he should do. He understood if he couldn't find a boat to take, his chances of evading capture would be slim.

Glen reached the water's edge. As he pulled himself up onto the paving stones, a searing pain went through his body like an electric shock. Biting his lip to suffocate a cry of pain, he lay on the ground, cold and wretched.

Although he had made it out of the lagoon, it felt as though the life was draining out of him like the water from his clothes. Raising his head, he saw a building a few feet distant. Open arches ran along the ground floor.

Calling on his last reserves of energy, he got to his feet and staggered over. He positioned himself out of sight behind one of the columns supporting an arch. His legs buckled and he slid to the floor.

CHAPTER 4

Glen didn't know how long he was there. He must have fallen asleep or passed out. Someone was tugging at his arm. He had no strength left to fight.
"Inglese?"
Glen nodded.
"You need to get up and come with me before the Germans find you. Here, take my hand."
Glen got up, wobbling like a drunkard. The good samaritan put his arm around Glen to steady him.
"Lean on me."
They set off slowly. The young man led Glen down an alley, then another, and maybe more. Glen didn't really notice. Putting one foot in front of the other demanded all his attention.
"Mama, Papa," whispered the man gently knocking on a wooden door by the side of a narrow canal.
When the door opened, he pushed Glen inside. Glen fell towards the couple. His helper grabbed him from behind.
"Help me get him up to the next floor so we can put him on the couch," said the other man.
Glen felt as if he was no longer himself, as if he

were somehow outside of his body. There was a buzzing in his head, and then nothing.

When he came to again, a bald man with round spectacles was standing above him with some sort of medical instrument in his hand. Like two fat centipedes, his eyebrows were large and thick.

Glen was naked from the waist up. He wondered if he was having a nightmare but it soon became all too apparent that he wasn't.

"We need to take the bullet out of you or you will die. I'm afraid we need to silence you. If you make a noise, you might be heard. Someone could report us. You can trust nobody these days." The man spoke in heavily accented English.

A woman, who Glen assumed to be the mother, unceremoniously pushed a cloth into Glen's mouth. Glen squirmed in agony while the man dug the instrument into his flesh to get at the bullet. The young man who had rescued him held his legs down and his mother squeezed Glen's hands in hers while she held them above his head. It was as if Glen was an animal tied up and awaiting slaughter.

"I'm sorry to hurt you like this, but it's the only way."

He poked inside Glen again with the instrument. Glen arched his back in torment.

"I have it. You can relax now."

The mother took the cloth from his mouth. Panting as though he'd just finished a long race, Glen said nothing. That had been the worst experience of his life. If a hell existed, it must be similar to this.

"Now I just need to apply a little antiseptic. We need to try and stop infection, and then I'll stitch you up."

The mother deftly pushed the cloth back into Glen's mouth before he could utter a word. He had no energy to resist.

He looked up at the mother. The gag muffled his cries of pain, first as the antiseptic was applied and then again as the needle repeatedly went in to stitch his red raw flesh back together. A tear ran down the woman's cheek to see him suffer so.

"You can sleep now," said the father.

When he awoke, the mother was sitting on a chair beside him. She smiled and touched his forehead. There was sorrow in her smile. Wrinkles, like a river delta of sadness, ran from the corner of her eyes and down her face. Her hair was white, not just grey, and prematurely so it seemed.

"Your poor mama. She must be so worried about you. And I can't even talk to you. I don't speak English."

"Io parlo italiano,"

"You speak Italian?" Her face lit up like sunshine. "Are you not English?"

"Yes, but I learned Italian working on ships. One of my crew mates was an Italian, from Genoa. He wanted to improve his English so I helped him. In return, he taught me Italian."

"He gave you a Genoan accent, but I'll forgive you

that. You speak it well. How are you feeling?"
"Sore."
"That's to be expected. You need to rest. You can stay here with us. We will hide you. My name is Signora Ferraro."
"Glen Butler. Your family saved my life. I'll be forever in your debt."
"We're only glad we could help someone who is trying to liberate us. You mustn't talk too much, you are exhausted. I will go make you some food."
Propped up on some cushions, Glen ate the splendid risotto which she had cooked. Just that one meal began to make him feel better.
Glen didn't remember much about the next few days. He slept most of the time. When awake, he fought to banish repeatedly re-living that awful night. The night when he had seen his comrades shot like rabbits. Each time he awoke his mind would drag him back there.
Signor Ferraro, a doctor at the hospital, examined him daily.
"Your progress is good. This evening you shall join us at the dinner table."
Glen felt awkward to see his plate was full but those of Signor and Signora Ferraro almost empty.
"Please take some of mine. I have too much."
"No, you need it more," said the Signora.
"Don't get better too quickly or you'll have to eat like us," joked her husband. "Everything is short these days. My hospital is fast running out of medical supplies. The Germans have taken all that

we didn't manage to hide away. The food markets are a shadow of their former selves. The Germans take first pick of everything. We can only hope the Allies drive them out soon.

"Mussolini has ruined us. But then we let him. Even I thought when he first took power that maybe it was a good thing. We were in chaos, and the people liked the order he brought. He made the trains run on time, so they tell us. He got us drunk on notions of glory, that Italy would become a great power. But then he started with his wars. Abyssinia, Libya, then Albania, Greece, Yugoslavia. Our other son, Giuseppe, God rest his soul, was forced to fight in Albania. He was killed by partisans."

He paused, suppressing his emotion. His wife laid her hand on the doctor's to comfort him.

"We Italians are no good at fighting. We are lovers, not fighters. Siding with Hitler has brought God's wrath down on us. When Italy surrendered to the Allies in the summer, the Germans invaded us making matters worse than ever. Do you know how the war is going? I'm sure a lot of what we hear isn't true."

"The Allies are making progress but it's slow going from what I know. The Germans have mounted a spirited defence. We're having to fight them every step of the way."

"Why were you here, behind the lines?"

"I'm afraid I'm not at liberty to say. It was a secret mission. I need to try and get back to Allied territory when I've recovered."

"That would be so dangerous. We could maybe get you across to the mainland, but once there you would be unlikely to survive. The Germans have said they will kill any families found to be harbouring the enemy so people would be reluctant to help you.

"And there are many fascist supporters out there, keen to pocket the rewards offered for catching Allied soldiers or partisans. If they found you, they would hand you over in the blink of an eye. We hear reports the Germans often shoot prisoners these days. It saves them the trouble of having to devote men and resources to looking after them and making sure that they don't escape."

"But I'm endangering you and your family by staying here."

"No, we are hiding our son Luca. If they find him, he will be forced into the army to go and die on the Russian front, and if he refuses he'll be sent to Germany as slave labour, and probably die there instead. As for us, we would doubtless be shot or sent off to Germany too. You can't make things any more perilous for us than they already are."

And so Glen stayed, though at times he wished he hadn't. The Ferraros couldn't have been kinder, but their house was still his prison. From the top floor, where he slept and spent most of his day, he could see along the narrow canal which ran outside their front door. Occasionally, gondolas would glide by transporting German officers and their Italian girlfriends. The laughter of happiness as they went past made his isolation that much harder to bear. They were living. He was marking time, his youth entombed and passing him by.

Across the terracotta tile rooftops, he could see several church towers and five grey domes close together, which Luca had told him was St. Mark's Cathedral. Glen longed to get out there and wander. How ironic that he should be spending so much time in this magnificent city but be unable to enjoy any of it.

The Ferraros assured him it wouldn't be long until the Allies would be here but the seasons came and went. Their intelligence was clearly faulty, or maybe they only said that to make him feel better.

At least the family loved books, owning many of them. Glen was able to spend his days reading and improving his Italian. He never succeeded in mastering Venetian, a strange mixture, he read, of French, German, Arabic and other languages. Fortunately, his hosts were diligent about speaking only in Italian in his presence.

Luca became Glen's student. "I want to learn English and go to America after this war ends. Will you teach me?"

"With pleasure, Luca. It's the least that I can do to repay you for saving my life."

"Do you know America?"

"No, but I've heard it's very beautiful."

"Especially the girls," laughed Luca.

Nineteen years old, Luca was a clone of his

father, save that he still had hair, and there was a brightness in his manner which his brother's death must have snuffed out in the doctor.

"What will you be when the war ends?" asked Glen.

"I want to be a doctor like Papa. I wanted to run away and join the partisans in the Dolomites, but my parents begged me not to. I know they fear my death, more than ever now that Giuseppe died. I made a deal with them that I would stay here, provided they let me run errands for the partisans in the city. That is why I go out at night. It's why I was out the night I found you. I know the hiding places in this city better than a rat. The Nazis will never catch me."

"Can I come with you sometime?"

"If it were only me at risk, I would happily say yes. But I have promised Mama and Papa not to take you. You don't know every nook and cranny. If we became separated, your chance of capture is extremely high. The Nazis would torture you until you confessed everything. I can't put my parents in still more danger. I hope you can understand that."

"I'm disappointed but of course I accept what you say."

Luca was a keen student and a quick learner.

"Do you think the American ladies will fall in love with my Italian accent?"

"Without a doubt," laughed Glen.

The two became close friends, Glen's only friend other than Luca's parents, and they were from a different generation.

"When liberation comes I'm going to show you the sights, and introduce you to the most beautiful Signorinas in all of Venice," promised Luca.

Tragedy struck during Glen's second winter of being trapped in the city.

CHAPTER 5

A knock at the front door one evening caused Glen's heart to miss a beat like it always did. He tore down the stairs from his room on the top floor, ready to hide in a gap under the floorboards on the floor below. He and Luca did so whenever there was an unexpected visitor.

The Ferraros would take their time to open the door to give him, and also Luca if he was at home, time to reach their hiding place.

"Father! Come in. How nice to see you. The doctor is still at the hospital."

Glen relaxed. It was only the priest.

His voice was soft, almost a whisper. Glen couldn't hear what he had to say. A haunting wail from Signora Ferraro told him all he needed to know.

Luca had ignored the curfew one time too many. His confidence, his youthful feeling of invulnerability had been too great.

The next morning, they brought his body home in an open coffin. All day long, friends and family arrived to offer their condolences. We can trust no one any longer the doctor had told him so Glen remained hidden in his room, unable to offer help or solace to the dear couple.

That evening after curfew and the prospect of no further visitors, he came down to be with the doctor and his wife. They sat impassively next to the coffin.

Luca was dressed in a white shirt and a black suit and tie. His dark hair was greased back and his face recently shaven. Glen had seen dead men before but that was in the heat of battle when death was all around, not a body displayed in someone's living room. Not someone so perfectly groomed and yet lifeless.

Luca had been so full of life and optimism. Glen's face crumpled. The doctor got up from his chair and came towards him. They put their arms around each other while they cried.

The following day, from his window up high, Glen observed the funeral procession proceed from the house. Neighbours lined the route in respectful silence before joining the back of the line. Before they reached the end of the street, fog enveloped them. After the church ceremony, Luca's coffin would be loaded onto a funeral boat and taken to the island of San Michele for burial.

When the Ferraros returned, Glen stayed in his room to give them privacy. Weary footsteps ascended the staircase, echoing off the walls like a mournful requiem.

"Why are you up here, Glen?" asked the doctor.

"I thought you might want time alone."

"No, you must come down. You are our son now, our only son."

They say the darkest hour is just before dawn. Dawn finally came a few weeks later in March 1945.

The sound of an explosion reverberated across the city, followed by several others. Seeing nothing in the east, Glen raced into the room next to his for a view of the west. Thick smoke rose from the docks to the south of the bridges connecting Venice to the mainland. Clapping with glee, he watched British aircraft dive vertically out of the sky.

It was a precision raid. Venetians clearly confident of that fact stood on surrounding rooftops watching the spectacle.

"God save the King!" cried Signora Ferraro when she returned from the market. It was the first time Glen had seen her smile since Luca's death two months ago. "By blowing up the docks, you've taught the Germans a lesson they won't forget in a hurry. And you didn't damage any of the buildings in our beautiful city, except for a few broken window panes. God bless you."

Codenamed Operation Bowler, because it was believed that if the historic buildings of Venice were destroyed, those in charge would be "bowler hatted" or dismissed, over fifty bombers attacked, diving from heights of up to ten thousand feet. They hit every boat in the harbour with only one plane shot down.

Signora Ferraro hugged Glen as he swept her off

her feet and twirled her around.

"Stop! You'll make me dizzy. We'll soon be liberated, Glen, soon. Those Germans have been shipping in supplies since the Allies took out the railways on the mainland. Now they'll be starved out. You've taken out a munitions dump too. They say you blew a hole in the dockside one hundred metres across."

Me, thought Glen. I've done nothing. I've hidden here in comfort and safety. 'You' were the brave pilots and the others risking their lives every day, not him.

Glen hoped freedom for the Venetians would come before starvation. The Nazis would be sure to deprive the local population of food before they themselves went hungry.

An even more momentous day came on 29 April 1945.

"Glen, get down here," cried Signora Ferraro. "The Germans have left. The Allies are coming!"

Quickly pulling on his clothes, he descended the stairs two at a time and almost fell at her feet.

"Go, go now. Join your people."

"I love you, Signora, I love you," he exclaimed as he hugged her.

"I love you too, Glen, but call me Mama."

"Mama," he said planting a kiss on her cheek. "I'll see you later."

Glen's face shone with happiness while he went outside for the first time in eighteen months and experienced the delight of fresh air. Finally free to walk about and to be seen, he pushed his way through the crowds heading towards the Piazzale Roma where the road bridge ended.

Allied armoured vehicles had already arrived. The soldiers jumped down from them to accept the adoration of the crowd. Men slapped them on the back or shook their hands. Excited young women threw their arms around them and kissed them with abandon. Nearby water taxis tooted their horns to offer a ride.

"Excuse me, sir, I'm Sub Lieutenant Butler," said Glen to an officer extracting himself from the embrace of a Venetian housewife. "I came here in November 1943 on a mission to blow up the causeway. The five others in my team were killed. I've been stuck hiding in this city ever since."

"It sounds like you deserve a break too. Come with us. We're off to requisition the Danieli with our New Zealand friends before the Yanks beat us to the best hotel in town like they did in Rome. There we were told the Hotel Excelsior had been reserved for us, but when we reached it the Americans told us to buzz off. Someone says they're right behind us with 'Hotel Danieli' signs on their trucks. Let's get on a boat and arrive first this time."

Glen marvelled at the sights, sounds, and colours while a local transported them in his boat down the Grand Canal. A liquid boulevard for the two hundred palazzi lining its shores.

Glen had only seen Venice close up in black and white, inanimate and somewhat dreary looking in books kept by the Ferraros. It was as though he had gone from watching a silent picture show of individual frames to Hollywood's latest and grandest all singing, all dancing technicolour production.

Boats sounded their horns, people waved from windows. As they passed under the Rialto bridge, Venetians threw flowers at them. Glen had indeed fallen out of a tower where evil had forced him to hide into some fantasy land, bubbling over with joy and goodwill. For today at least, thoughts of death, loss, and revenge had been cast aside.

While they progressed, the palazzi along the canal grew grander. Beneath one, a man stood precariously on the shoulders of a gondolier, pulling at the hated swastika flag of their oppressor, which was still draped from a window. The crowd on the Accademia bridge clapped with approval as, with a final wrench, the man pulled it free. They then roared with laughter when he lost his balance and toppled into the water, cheering as he surfaced and waved at them with a grin on his face, leaving the flag to float down the canal like a dead basilisk.

The perfectly proportioned Santa Maria della Salute to their right presaged their entry into the lagoon. Built to thank God for deliverance from the plague in the seventeenth century, its bells rang now to celebrate the deliverance of the city from the grip of tyranny.

Their boat turned left. Glen had thought nothing

could surpass the Grand Canal until he saw St. Mark's Cathedral, the Campanile, and the pink hues of the Doges' Palace with its arabesque arches. Two tall columns stood in the foreground close to the water. Atop one was the winged lion, the symbol of Venice, and on the other Saint Theodore, the patron saint of Venice before the arrival of the alleged relics of Saint Mark, spirited out from Alexandria, had usurped Theodore from that position. A spear in hand, Theodore stands on what looks like a crocodile, but is claimed to represent a dragon he is alleged to have slain.

The eclectic scene caused Glen to recall Charles Dickens' description of the city:

"Opium couldn't build such a place, and enchantment couldn't shadow it forth in a vision."

CHAPTER 6

Their boat moored in front of an ochre palace. It looked like that of a Sultan. Its wooden shutters were pinned back. The stone surrounds of the windows curved to a point, redolent of Istanbul. A large balcony on the second floor bore cream coloured pillars of the same design as the Doge's Palace in a quatrefoil pattern, like enormous stone keys. Above them, in gold lettering, was the word, Danieli, the most famous hotel in Venice.

Four truncated columns with pointed tops, as though shrunken minarets, adorned the roof. From flagpoles leaning forwards from the third floor, four flags flapped in the breeze. The Italian tricolor, the Venetian flag of red, with its winged lion in gold and, no doubt hastily run up that very morning, the Union Jack and the Stars and Stripes. Fearing this was all but a dream and he would soon wake up back in that small and claustrophobic attic room, Glen pinched himself to confirm his reality.

He followed the officer and other soldiers off the boat and through the revolving wooden

doors towards reception. They were greeted by walls of dappled pink and grey marble, arches and columns. A gothic red-carpeted staircase at the back ascended back and forth. Above them was open space all the way to the top of the building. Glen stood open mouthed, stunned by the opulence of the establishment.
"Are we a fish, Butler?"
"No, sir."
"Well, stop gaping like one." The officer approached the man standing behind the reception desk of dark wood, polished until it shone. "We're requisitioning the hotel."
"And how will you be paying, sir? Our last guests left in rather a hurry, and without settling their account."
The officer's previously jovial face became puce faster than a chameleon can change colour. He grabbed the receptionist by his shirt collar and pulled him forwards until he must have been standing on tiptoes.
"My men and I have spent the last year and a half clawing our way inch by inch up your fucking country to free you and your fellow countrymen from a mess that you created. Thousands of our troops have died, and thousands more no longer have arms or legs, so don't you ask me how we will pay."
He let go and the man adjusted his collar in an attempt to recover his dignity.
"Of course, sir. My porters will take you up to the

rooms. Please advise them who should have the best ones."

Glen stood to one side. He hadn't fought his way through hell to get here. Yes, he'd been a prisoner for eighteen months, but his jailers had been kind and compassionate. He might be thinner than he once was, though he was better fed than many. Glen turned to go.

"Butler, just exactly where do you think you are going?"

"Sir, I don't deserve this."

"Nonsense. I know about your raid. You showed as much bravery as any of us. I can send you off to join your ship immediately, or I can let you have a few days R&R. What's it to be?"

Glen grinned. "Yes, I didn't think so. And I'll have a fresh uniform sent up to your room. You look a bloody disgrace man."

Glen was allocated a side room overlooking the Rio del Vin, its waters a mesmerising translucent turquoise in the sunshine.

That evening, Glen joined the throngs celebrating in Piazza San Marco. The US army was here too now. They had a jazz band playing in the centre of the square. It was as though New Orleans had twinned herself with Venice, sending her joyful music as a gift.

A young Italian woman tapped him on the shoulder.

"You dance, soldier?"

Glen delighted her by responding in Italian.

"Not very well."
"That doesn't matter. It's the passion that counts."
She placed one hand on his shoulder and took hold of his hand with the other. Glen revelled in her smell of perfume and enticing femininity. She was a ravishing beauty like her city. He was here in Venice, dancing under the moon. Could a day get any better than this?
"Mind if I cut in, buddy?"
Before he had time to answer she had let go of him and was dancing with the GI. Glen had a ball that night. Free drinks flowed, numerous dancing partners, and come morning...ouch.
Glen's head ached as though it had a fault line running through it which would split apart like the San Andreas at any moment. He got out of bed and went across to the sink. With cupped hands, he drank water and splashed some on his face.
A heavy knock on the door made his head hurt more. He was presented with a uniform, a cap, and a coat. In the pocket was money and a handwritten note:
'Down payment on unpaid wages due since November 1943.'
Glen got dressed and went out. Like curious sea monsters, amphibious vehicles were coming out of the lagoon onto the Riva degli Schiavoni, but otherwise it was quiet while the city slept off the greatest collective hangover in its history.
There was something which Glen wanted to do. He threaded his way through the streets until

reaching a market. There he bought some food and flowers. Asking passers-by for directions, he navigated his way to the Ferraros' house.

"Glen! How handsome you look in your new uniform. And what is this?" said Signora Ferraro.

"I'm sorry it can't be more. When I get paid I'll send you money for all that rent I owe you."

"You will do no such thing. Where are you staying?"

"The Danieli."

"Oh, my word. That is luxury indeed."

"They'll be shipping me out in a few days."

"Then you must come to dinner this evening."

Though the Ferraros fought to be jolly, the cosiness of the candle light and the feast Signora Ferraro had prepared couldn't mask the sadness of the occasion for them. The ghost of their two sons hung unspoken but loud in the flickering shadows, and now Glen too would be gone from their lives.

The doctor would bury himself in his work but what about the Signora? Glen wondered how she coped in this big house, each room so full of memories. Sadly, she was just one of millions across the world having to bear loss from this awful war. The fighting would soon be over but the war to conquer grief would never end for some.

"Write to us, don't forget us. God sent you to us."

"You have saved our lives too. Someone to care for when our sons were taken away."

Their parting words crushed Glen. Like a balloon bursting, the hedonism of yesterday's celebrations deflated quickly.

Glen's mood was morose while he wandered back towards the hotel through the labyrinth of alleys, crossing the small bridges over the canals. From yesterday's high, he had fallen into a deep low.

He thought of the hate and destruction which had run rampant across Europe in an orgy of violence unparalleled in its history, the human race its victim. He thought of his dead colleagues who would never see a tomorrow. But he didn't want revenge. Everyone needed to get off this wicked merry-go-round that had consumed the continent and get back to living their lives, in peace.

Glen certainly wanted to be free to live his. Since 1939, his life hadn't been his own, and for the last year and a half, his world had been but a single room. He was eighteen when the war started and now he was twenty-four. Six years taken, years he could never get back. They should have been the best years of his life, not years of seeing men blown to pieces, screaming for help he wasn't able to give.

Shouts up ahead interrupted his thoughts. When he got closer, he could make out the words. Whore. Nazi whore.

CHAPTER 7

The shouting appeared to be coming from around the corner ahead of him. He followed the source into a small square.

An angry group stood around a young woman seated on a wooden dining chair beneath the harsh light of a lamp on the wall behind her. She had her arms across her chest. Her dress and bra had been ripped from her shoulders. An elderly woman was cutting her hair without care, the black locks falling to the ground.

Other women took it in turns to move forward and slap her face. Blood ran from her nostrils. Men spat on her. Both sexes continued hurling obscenities at her. She was like a gazelle cornered by a pride of lions while they toyed with her before moving in for the kill.

"Enough!" Glen heard himself cry out even to his own surprise. Something inside him had gone off, something which he hadn't been able to control.

Momentarily struck dumb by his intervention, the crowd turned to face him.

"Who are you?" demanded one

"I'm a British soldier, and I order you to stop."

"Leave us alone. This is none of your business. She's a traitor, a German officer's mistress. She betrayed her country. You know the penalty for treason."

"Hasn't there been enough killing? The war is over. It's time to stop."

"Get out of here. We don't want to hurt you. You're not our enemy."

"No, I'm not. But I will be if you don't comply. My friends died to free you. They didn't sacrifice their lives so that you could behave like the Nazis. I'm not leaving without her."

Cold sweat ran down Glen's sides from under his arms. His Adam's apple rose and fell while he swallowed hard. He moved forwards, fighting against his desire to turn and run. The crowd parted. He held out his hand to the woman.

"Come with me."

The woman looked around as though waiting for permission from the crowd.

"Now," urged Glen.

She got up and followed while Glen walked backwards. He was wary of the crowd's apparently subdued mood. He could almost taste the tension in the air. Things could change at any moment, only one had to be willing to take the lead and the rest would surely follow.

The moment they were out of the square, he asked her to hurry. She ran as best she could, trying to keep up with him while she struggled to cover her bare breasts. Once they had gone around the next corner, he stopped to let her catch up.

"Here, take my coat and cap."

She took them, turning her back on him to put the coat on.

"Where do you live?" asked Glen.

"Nowhere now."

"We'll go to the Danieli then."

"The Danieli? I have no money."

"I have a room there. You can stay with me while we work out what to do."

He led her in a back way. They skulked up the stairs like foxes on the prowl. Unlocking the door to his room, he stood back for her.

She entered and stood by the cupboard, pulling the top of the coat tightly around her. Her scalp, most of which was now visible, bore cuts from where the scissors had been wielded too closely. Only a few clumps of hair remained.

When Glen approached her, she moved back towards the window.

"It's okay, I'm not going to hurt you. I rescued you, didn't I?" She avoided his gaze, looking down at the floor." Did you want to use the bathroom? Have a bath?" She nodded. "You'll find a dressing gown behind the door."

When she emerged, she seemed much calmer. The fear had gone from here eyes. She'd shaven off the odd pieces of hair that remained on her head.

"I hope you don't mind. I used your razor."

"You can sit on the bed," said Glen taking the chair

next to it. "Is it true what they said?"

"It's true I had a German boyfriend once, if that's what you mean."

"Why?"

"That's really none of your business."

An awkward silence followed.

"Has he just gone?"

"No, he left a few months ago. Look, thank you for what you did."

"I've seen enough brutality in the last few years to last me a lifetime. It's time for the world to heal, not go on making things worse. What's your name?"

"Alessandra. And you?"

"Glen. Glen Butler. Where are you from?"

"Verona."

"Do you have family there?"

"My mother."

"Then I'll see what I can do to get you back there. You can have the bed. Chuck me one of the blankets. I'll sleep on the floor."

You idiot, Glen scolded himself, while he lay waiting for sleep to come. You could have got yourself killed tonight. You were one lucky sod that they didn't turn on you. You wouldn't have stood a chance.

The following morning, Glen watched her while she slept. Alessandra looked so peaceful, her eyes shut, last night's look of trauma gone or hidden. She now had a black eye as the bruising came out, and her nose looked broken, swollen and slightly bent. The pillow was marked with dried blood stains from the cuts on her head.

He wrote her a note to say he would be back later. Alessandra was sitting on the bed, her legs tucked under her when he returned.

"I've brought some things for you. A dress, and a scarf for your head. And I got you something to eat."

"Thank you, Glen. I am grateful. You must give me your address so I can repay you when I have some money."

"No need. Let's just say I'm returning a little of the generosity others have shown to me. Go in the bathroom and try the dress on."

"It fits," he said when she came out of the bathroom.

Glen noticed for the first time how attractive she must be behind those bruises and her bare scalp. The pale green dress, buttoned up the front and fitted at the waist, showcased her figure. His stomach turned over and his pulse raced.

For the second time in twenty-four hours, he found himself doing something he hadn't thought he ever would. His near death experience and being deprived of his liberty had killed any caution he once felt, had made him impulsive. He had a need to seize the moment, it might never come again.

Placing his hands gently on her shoulders, he moved his mouth to hers. She moved her head back, away from him. He too took a step backwards, embarrassed for taking advantage of the situation.

"I'm sorry."

"It's all right Glen, but can we close the curtains first. I feel so ugly in the daylight."

The darkness created by the blackout curtains hid them but they found each other. There was no need to see. It heightened their sense of touch. Each needed that moment of tenderness, using the other to feel human again.

Afterwards each lay there feeling guilt, not for what they'd just done, but for what had gone before in their lives. How they had lived and others hadn't.

They remained in the room that day and night. Tomorrow both of them would need to resume their lives and find their future, but for now they could forget their worries and use each other to escape their demons temporarily.

The next morning, Glen walked her to Piazzale Roma to find transport. Alessandra locked her arm in his and kept her head down. The scarf hid her scalp but not her identity. They found a bus going to Padua.

"Here's money for your fare and a bit extra. Hopefully that will get you to Verona."

"Thank you, Glen. I'll never forget you."

But she didn't look back when she boarded the bus, and Glen didn't wait to wave her off.

CHAPTER 8

Glen was released from the Navy in September 1945. Not knowing what he wanted to do, he drifted into a bank trainee management programme. So it was that in early 1946, he found himself lodging in the coastal town of Swanage in Dorset, posted there by his employer.

If Venice had seemed drab during his two winters there, Swanage took drabness to a new level. For weeks under unbroken cloud, angry grey seas pounded the beach, the surf leaping high in the air as it slammed into the seawall. Rain blew in horizontally. It was too windy to use an umbrella and Glen was often soaked when he got back to his landlady's house at the end of the work day.

"Venice, you say. Well, maybe it's pretty, but those foreign places aren't for me. All that strange food they eat, and I bet those canals pong something terrible in summer. Ernie took me to the Italian in Poole for dinner once. Never again. You must be so glad to be home. You just can't beat this country, can you? I've cooked you some lovely tripe for supper."

"Mmm," feigned Glen.

The edible lining of a cow's stomach wasn't quite what he'd hoped for. Still, with rationing now stricter than during the war itself, good meals weren't easy to come by. His mind drifted back to Italy. Even with the limited ingredients which she had access to, Signora Ferraro cooked tastier meals than Mrs Bains' best.

Glen wasn't happy in Swanage but resolved to give it a few more months. If things didn't improve, he would seek a job in London. This small, provincial town held little attraction for a young man.

The rain did stop, and come spring the English countryside transformed itself from an ugly duckling into a swan. Hedgerows greened and white blossom weighed down hawthorn trees. Yellow daffodils gave a bright pop of colour, and the grass on the hillsides changed from the washed-out colours of winter to a luxuriant green. In the fields, lambs jumped as though they were coiled springs being released. A brief period of cuteness before they became sheep, whose legs appeared too thin to support their bodies, and whose black, rectangular pupil on an opaque amber eyeball gave them an alien appearance.

Glen took walks up the paths which climbed the hills on either side of the town. White chalk cliffs dropped into the sea which sparkled in the bright sunlight. Inhaling the invigorating air, he would lie down on the grass up on the cliff tops. There, sheltered from the wind, he welcomed the warmth on his face.

Out there in the blue, beyond the horizon, was northern France, and a road that could lead him back to Italy. Seeing inside Pandora's box of continental Europe had made Glen restless. Maybe he would travel. Go back to Venice and take in the other sights of Italy, perhaps meet a beautiful Italian woman and marry her. A life of thrills and possibilities, an enticing world away from dull predictability.

A visit to the local dance relegated such thoughts to a maybe one day, although it hadn't been an auspicious start.

As he carried a glass of beer back to his table, Glen tripped. The brown liquid went flying, drenching the dress of a young woman seated nearby.

"You clumsy oaf!"

"I'm sorry but if you hadn't left your handbag on the floor, I wouldn't have caught my foot in it."

"So you're blaming me?"

"No, but...can I buy you a drink to make up for it?"

"No. I'm leaving, I can't sit around in a wet dress all evening smelling of beer, can I?"

Sensing many pairs of judging eyes burrowing into the back of his head, Glen departed also.

Walking down the high street a few days later, he saw her. Impulsively, he bought a bunch of roses from a nearby flower stall and hurried past her before turning around to block her way.

"Look, I'm sorry about the other night. I hope you can accept these as an apology."

Her look was inscrutable. It didn't seem as though his olive branch would be taken. Then, like the sun moving out from behind a cloud, she smiled and Glen was smitten.

"Apology accepted."

"Would you care for a cup of tea?"

"So long as you promise not to pour it all over me."

Dora had a sweet, unaffected personality with a healthy dose of humour and self-deprecation. A smile was rarely absent from her face or laughter from her voice. For Glen, her green eyes danced like the fresh grass of early summer.

Cliff walks became even better. There was Dora's hand to hold, her hair to smell, and those sweet lips to kiss. Europe could stay over the horizon. The empty hole in Glen's life had been filled.

By the following year, their plans were well advanced. It was now June and their wedding was only two weeks away. Glen was going to surprise her, a honeymoon in Paris paid for with his back wages from the war. Dora wanted nothing more than to be a wife and mother, and had already persuaded Glen what the name of their first born should be.

He had found them a place to rent in the hilltop village of Kingston. It was only a few miles to reach their jobs in town, a cycle for him and a short bus ride for Dora. The furniture which they'd bought had been delivered, and Greg would move in next week. It was exciting, he had never had a home of his own, and better than that he was madly in love.

The stone cottage with latticed windows looked over the open countryside towards the ruins of Corfe Castle which sat on its own hill a couple of miles distant. When shrouded in early morning mist, the castle appeared to float on the lowland fog, like something out of the tales of King Arthur and the Knights of the Round Table.

Glen and Dora had found their own Camelot here in Dorset. Life was perfection. For a moment.

Glen should have realised that it would contain unexpected news. After all, the Ferraros knew his address. The envelope his landlady handed him bearing an Italian stamp had been redirected, originally addressed to him care of the British Navy. But Glen's mind was elsewhere. He was in a hurry to get ready to be at Dora's parents' house by six o'clock for dinner.

While he scanned the neat handwriting, Glen pushed his hand back through his hair, again and again

Daughter. Orphanage. Those two words changed everything.

CHAPTER 9

1931

The nun's hand on his head was firm. She pushed his face down onto the cold wetness. The stench of urine was overwhelming.

"You'll keep your head there until I tell you that you can move it. It will remind you not to wet the bed again."

How long did she leave him there? Ten minutes, twenty? It felt forever until a sweaty hand pulled him up by the ear.

"Now go wash your face, and get ready quickly or you'll be punished for being late for prayers."

Blinking back tears, Glen scuttled off. He would never give these witches the satisfaction of thinking they had got the better of him. He could cry at night, silently, when the lights were out.

He resented his mother for dying. If she hadn't, he would still be safe, not trapped in this place. And as for God, he hated him. The nuns told them God loved everyone. But how could that be when God left him here with his evil handmaidens. And hadn't God wanted his mother to join him? Taken her away, even though Glen needed her more.

She was, they told him, in a better place, but what about him? There was no nourishing, caring figure in his life. The only women he had contact with were unfeeling harridans. They didn't even look like women. Their hair was hidden, their faces bore no makeup, and they smelled of nothing.

He and his friend Dominic made plans to escape. They would run away. They could find barns to sleep in and steal food by slipping through kitchen windows left open. They would run until they reached the coast and stowaway aboard a ship.

Dominic said they should go to America. There, children got everything they wanted, he said. He had seen it for real, at the cinema before he got sent to the orphanage.

One evening, they climbed out of the window after lights out. Taking a ladder from the shed, they got over the wall. They jumped with joy. Nothing would stop them now.

"How do we find the coast?" asked Glen.

"We go south."

"Which way is that?"

"Where the sun is at midday, stupid."

"Don't call me stupid."

Glen punched him and they fell onto the damp grass, wrestling.

"You've broken my nose," cried Dominic.

"It's only a nose bleed, you cry baby. Come on. We better get going."

A full moon lit their way. Was that in the south,

they wondered. They followed it anyway. As the night wore on, their enthusiasm began to wane. It was chilly now and they were both tired.

"Look, there's a barn over there."

Glen cautiously opened the barn's heavy door, trying desperately to keep the loud creaking sound to a minimum. The farm house wasn't far away. A dog barked.

Creatures flew at them, squawking. The boys put their hands over their faces and screamed as feathery wings touched them while whatever monsters they had disturbed went past them. Then all was quiet again.

They went inside and closed the barn door and lay down on some straw. It was much softer than their beds in the orphanage, almost like floating on a cloud. They were asleep in seconds.

Shafts of sunlight coming through the cracks in the wood woke them. The farmer looked scarier than the nuns, standing there and pointing his rifle at them.

"You little hooligans are staying here until the police arrive. You let my hens out. The foxes got four of them."

By late afternoon and after a firm talking to from the policeman, they were back at the orphanage, standing in front of the Mother Superior. She was the most evil witch of them all.

"Put out your hands."

Her voice would have cracked ice. She whacked them repeatedly with a cane until their hands were red and stung intensely.

"You boys are out of control. I'm sending you to orphanages run by the Brothers. Different ones, mind you. You two can't be trusted to be together."

This time Glen couldn't hold back the tears. Dominic was his best friend, his only friend.

"Stop bubbling, boy."

The Mother Superior thwacked him on the backside with the cane for good measure.

The monks were joyless like the nuns. The boys were all older than Glen, though by the time he reached twelve he was as old as new boys joining. Glen kept a low profile and for the most part managed to stay out of trouble. He planned for the day when he would get out of here and could go off to sea, to a place they would never be able to find him.

One morning he lingered in the shower. It was winter so the water was at least luke warm, not cold like during the summer. The other boys had gone.

He sensed someone was staring at him. It was Brother Patrick. The man didn't look away when Glen looked at him. Embarassed, Glen turned his back on him and quickly finished washing.

"Come and see me after breakfast," said the Brother.

What have I done now, thought Glen as he knocked nervously on his door.

"Do you like chocolate?"

"Yes."

"I have some. Here, take it. But keep it a secret, our secret."

Glen was confused by this show of kindness but he took it anyway. Sweets were a rare treat here.

Next week, the same happened again. The third week Glen smiled before entering, at last he'd found a Brother who seemed kind.

"Sit down, Glen."

Brother Patrick rose from his chair and came to where Glen was sitting.

"I've been very generous with you, haven't I? Now it's your turn."

He grabbed Glen's hand and pulled it towards his cassock. Glen flinched but the friar's grip was strong.

"Tell anyone about this and I'll tell them you're lying. That you're a wicked, wicked boy and need to be punished. Understand?"

Glen nodded his head in submission.

Two weeks passed. Glen began to believe it was over, a nightmare he could try and forget. But it wasn't.

"Come with me," whispered the friar poking him awake in his bed one night.

Sneaking back into bed an hour later, Glen resolved to run away immediately. He had to get away from that man.

This time he succeeded. He made it to London and the docks.

Glen had never been somewhere with so many people. He could be invisible here. No one gave him a second look. Huge vessels towered above him as he walked along the quayside.

"Do you know who I can ask about a job?" said Glen to a man walking towards a ship's gangplank with a large bag slung over his shoulder.

"Him over there," he said pointing. "He's the captain."

Glen approached the man. He looked imposing but not frighteningly so in his navy blue uniform and shining gold buttons.

"Excuse me, sir. I'm looking for a job on your ship."

"How old are you?"

"Fifteen," lied Glen.

"You're in luck. I'm short of a deckhand. We're off to India, via the Suez Canal. Follow me."

India. They would never catch him now. When the boat pulled away from the dock, Glen let out a cry of sheer delight. He couldn't remember the last time he had done that.

CHAPTER 10

1947

Glen sat down on his bed and read again the letter which was written in Italian, hoping a second reading might make the words change.

Dear Glen
I hope this letter finds you well.
This will come as a surprise. You have a daughter. A beautiful daughter. She was born 5 February 1946. The nuns have named her Isabella.
As an unmarried mother, I wasn't allowed to keep her. It breaks my heart to think she will be brought up in the orphanage. There are so many orphans here now after the war that they don't have the time or money to care for them properly. I worry so much about her future if she stays there.
If you haven't married, I beg you to consider coming here to marry me so I may take Isabella out of the orphanage and give her a home. I would do everything in my power to be a good wife and make you happy.
In hope,

Alessandra Faccini

Appartamento 5
Via Garibaldi
Verona

Glen put his head in his hands. He loved Dora so much. He was so happy, happier than he'd ever been, happier than he had ever thought he could be.

But there was only one solution to the dilemma which he now faced. He had no choice. He couldn't leave a daughter of his in an orphanage. He knew what those places were like. He couldn't betray her. Trembling, he knocked on the door of the grey stone Victorian house.

"You're half an hour late," scolded Dora. "Whatever's the matter, Glen? You look terrible."

"I need to tell you something."

Dora pulled the front door to and stepped outside.

"I don't know what to say," said Dora after he explained.

"I'm so sorry, Dora. You're the last person in the world I want to hurt."

She looked directly at him. Her look wasn't one of understanding, more one of disdain.

"Go, Glen, just go. Before I make a fool of myself."

She ran up the steps and inside.

Two weeks later Alessandra was waiting when the train from Milan pulled in to Verona's station. She waved hesitantly and waited for him to walk over to her. She had radiant black hair now, all the way to her shoulders and she was wearing a blue frock

and holding a small bunch of flowers. There was a bump in her nose from where it had been broken.
"I cannot thank you enough, Glen."
"Where do we go?" asked Glen listlessly.
"The town hall."
It was an imposing building next to the Roman Arena. Its steps were wide, the width of the eight spaced columns holding up the grand entrance. A building so magnificent that Glen should have felt something.
The wedding was an unmemorable affair. No bridesmaids, no family, no friends. It couldn't have been more different to what he and Dora had planned. Glen repeated the words he was asked to without conviction, placed the ring on her finger he had brought without looking at her, and signed the papers placed in front of him without attention.The man officiating raised his eyebrows and rolled his eyes at his colleague when the couple departed.
"What now?" asked Glen when they exited back into the bright sunshine.
"I've booked us a hotel here in Piazza Bra. Then tomorrow, I thought we could go and collect Isabella."
The Piazza was attractive. A garden of cypress and pine trees in the centre, the Arena to one side, and a long line of restaurants and hotels at one edge with green canopies protecting customers from the hot sun.
Their room at the hotel overlooked the

nineteen hundred year old Arena, an elliptical amphitheatre, which had even survived an earthquake in the twelfth century. Its two tiers of giant arches all the way around it made it truly spectacular.

In Roman times, it was a venue for gladiators and wild animals to fight and die. Its present use was much more pleasant. That evening, the passion of an opera being performed within the Arena floated through their open window. It should have been romantic, a perfect night. Their wedding night.

Glen stood staring out of the window, a far away look in his eyes. Alessandra came over to join him. He didn't reciprocate when she put her arms around him and resisted the soft touch of her lips.

"I'm sorry, I can't. I need to take a walk."

Glen found a bench to sit on. The night was blissfully warm. Couples strolled hand in hand, all taking advantage of the free music. They couldn't see the performance, but they could feel it as they let it flow through them and capture their emotions.

Glen yearned to be here with Dora. She was his Juliet, in this city of Romeo and Juliet.

He stayed long after the opera finished, until the absence of others told him it was late, almost dawn. Alessandra was fast asleep when he slipped stealthily into bed, not wanting to wake her, not wanting to have to explain anything.

CHAPTER 11

"How long were you with Isabella until she was put in the orphanage?" asked Glen while they drank coffee at the pavement cafe in front of their hotel the next morning.

"They would only let me stay with her a few months while I breastfed her. I lived at the orphanage. Then one day the nuns came in to take her and told me I must leave and wouldn't be able to see her again. It was awful. Our beautiful little girl snatched away from me. Nobody to love her."

"Why didn't you write sooner?"

"I didn't think I had the right. I thought my heartache for her would pass but it kept getting stronger. I believe you too will fall in love with her when you meet her."

While they sat waiting at the orphanage, Glen tapped his fingers on the arms of the wooden chair. The place made him anxious. Memories which he'd never wanted to revisit had played havoc with his mind since getting that letter.

Isabella would be lucky. She would be too young to remember ever having been in an orphanage.

She wouldn't have to endure the childhood he had experienced. He was at least glad about that.

A nun asked them to follow her. They went into a side room and sat once again while she examined their papers.

"All seems in order. I just need you to sign here, and then I can reunite you with your daughter."

The dormitory must have contained over thirty young children in cots. It was an austere, clinical space. A shiver from Glen's past ran down his spine. No pictures of fairies or teddy bears, train engines or elephants hung on the walls. Instead, Jesus on the cross and a portrait of the Virgin Mary holding her baby looked down upon the infants.

"We must be quiet. They're taking their nap," whispered the nun. "Here is Isabella."

She lay uncovered, her head to one side while she sucked her thumb vigorously. Like a cherub, her face was round and full. Chestnut curls covered her head. She was dressed in what must once have been a white smock when its first owner had worn it. Now it had a sallow tint to it.

"You may pick her up."

Alessandra leaned over the rail and gently raised her. "Glen, meet your daughter."

As she handed the little girl to him, Isabella opened her eyes momentarily but the effort was too much and she closed them again, slumping forward onto Glen's shoulder. Her snuffles and the warmth of her body melted his heart.

Signora Faccini, Alessandra's mother, smiled to see

the child when they arrived at her apartment.
"Mama, this is Glen."
"Pleased to meet you…er…"
"You may call me Signora Faccini."
She gave Glen no smile. Her countenance seemed as austere as the widow's dress code she observed.
"I need to change her," said Alessandra. "I won't be long."
Glen and her mother shared an awkward silence.
"You may sit."
The room was sombre, the shutters closed to keep out the sun. Dark furniture crowded the small space. On the wall hung a photograph of a man.
"Is that Signor Faccini?"
"Yes. He died in the war."
"I'm sorry. It must have been very hard for you and Alessandra."
She ignored his condolences. "So you finally decided to do the decent thing."
"I'm afraid I didn't know."
"Or do you mean that you'd had your pleasure so you didn't care."
Alessandra returned with Isabella.
"Take that baby into the kitchen. She'll need feeding, and make your husband some coffee and bring it to him in here."
Glen remained in the living room, alone, exiled by his mother-in-law.
"So what are your plans? You can stay here a few days of course while you search for an apartment in Verona," said the Signora that evening while

they ate dinner together.

"I must return to England tomorrow. I will send for Alessandra and Isabella as soon as I can. That is just as soon as the immigration papers are finalised."

"What! You disgrace my daughter, and now you take her and my granddaughter away from me. Have you no heart? Why can't you come here to Verona to live? You speak Italian, after all."

"Mama, please. He has a good job in England. We will come and visit you every year."

Her mother stood up and lifted her hands dramatically as if calling for divine intervention.

"Every year? See my granddaughter but once a year? How can you do this to me? Your poor father would turn in his grave. I'm going to bed, my heart is broken."

CHAPTER 12

Early the next morning, Glen kissed Isabella goodbye and gave Alessandra a perfunctory peck on the cheek. Signora Faccini remained in bed, sulking.

Rain ran like tears down the window of the steam train as it approached Swanage. Glen took the bus out to Kingston. The low hanging cloud oppressed him. The cottage was damp and unwelcoming. He wondered what to do about the furniture he and Dora had bought. He wrote Dora a note and rode his bicycle down to Swanage. He hoped that no one would open the door. Glen popped the note through the letter box and walked briskly down the path towards the gate.

"Glen?" He halted and turned.

"Mrs Willoughby. I left a note for Dora. I wanted to ask her about the furniture we bought."

"I don't think that she'll be worried about it. Do what you think best. Dora's gone. She's moved to Dorchester. She's living with her aunt. Fred and I thought it would be easier for her if she got away, started again somewhere fresh."

"I'm very sorry, Mrs Willoughby."

"You did the right thing. Can't leave your little girl in an orphanage, can you. I hope you'll all be very happy. Goodbye now." She shut the door abruptly.

Glen resumed work. The Home Office said that it would be a few months until they would issue the necessary documents.

He decorated the spare bedroom with pink wallpaper. In a shop window in Swanage, he saw a rocking horse which he carried awkwardly under one arm while he cycled up the steep hill home, frequently stopping to change arms. Cows put their heads over the dry stone walls to watch him pass. Transporting the doll and teddy bear that he bought was much easier. They fitted in the basket on the front of his bike.

A letter arrived in late summer to tell him that his wife and child could pick up their papers from the British Consulate in Milan.

When she saw her bedroom, Isabella clapped her hands together with joy and jumped up and down. She heaved herself onto the rocking horse and giggled when she promptly fell off the other side.

"Was there someone you loved?" asked Alessandra while they lay in bed that night.

"It's in the past. I don't want to talk about it."

But Glen saw Dora's face when he made love to Alessandra.

They say arranged marriages work as couples grow to love each other. Glen wondered if a forced marriage would be the same. Alessandra was a nice person, attentive and undemanding. If she needed more from him than he was able to give, she never said. Glen waited for love to grow. Isabella had already stolen his heart, and both parents found a happiness in loving her. The years passed quickly.

Glen glowed as Isabella's hero. What better time is there in a father's life when your little daughter idolises you. She wanted to be with him constantly. Like a faithful puppy, she would skip by his side, holding his hand when they went on walks.

Their favourite route was to take the farm track down to the sea to a cove called Chapman's Pool. In winter, they would throw pebbles into the sea and, in summer, paddle about and splash each other. Isabella would stubbornly refuse to climb the track back up to the house and demand a piggyback.

When she became heavier, Glen often chose the level walk out of the village to the cliff at Hounstout, and refused to go down the steep path to the beach unless she promised to walk back up the track to Kingston unaided. From the ridge they kept to on their way to the clifftop, they could look down upon the grey stone stately home, Encombe House, in the valley below to the west.

"Who lives in that big house?" asked Isabella.

"The local landowner, but once upon a time a princess lived there," answered Glen. "She fell in love with the dashing young captain of a passing ship who sought shelter in the house one stormy night. Her parents, who wanted her to marry the old king who lived in Corfe Castle, refused to give permission to a marriage with the captain.

"Each day the princess would sit on the clifftops looking out to sea. One day she saw his boat pass by again. It struck rocks and began to sink. She hurried to the beach and rowed out in a small boat to save him but it was too late. Overcome with grief, she jumped over the side.

"The merpeople took pity on them both and turned them into merman and mermaid. Now they live happily ever after under the ocean. They say that if you look really long and hard you can sometimes see them jump out of the water for a moment before they disappear back down into the depths."

"More, more," cried Isabella with delight.

As she grew, they extended their walks until she even managed the steep path from Chapman's Pool up to the austere Norman chapel at St. Aldhelm's Head. Here, the wind blew unimpeded and the tidal races stretched out to sea, creating a maelstrom on the surface where passing yachts would rise and fall at steep angles.

Alessandra didn't venture out of the house often, though with Glen's help her English became quite fluent. The farthest she went was to Swanage on the bus but even there she became reluctant to go after she overheard a couple of women discussing her when she passed them.

"Look, that's her. His Italian harlot."

"I know. It's shocking what they'll do to get over

here."

Alessandra rarely complained about her situation. Isabella was happiness enough for her. While Glen clearly didn't love his wife, he was considerate and an excellent father.

Sometimes she couldn't hold back from expressing her dislikes, such as Glen's obsession for watching television programmes about the war.

"Turn that off. The war ended years ago. Anyway, Isabella shouldn't be seeing such things."

"No, I won't. It's good for the younger generation to learn about the concentration camps to make sure that it never happens again."

Alessandra left the room and went upstairs.

Every August, she and Isabella spent a month in Verona visiting her Nonna. For years, Glen pleaded lack of money and that his boss always took time off in August as excuses for being unable to join them.

One summer, he relented and joined them for two weeks. Signora Faccini refrained from verbal assaults but she was a woman who didn't need speech to express her true feelings. Her frown or deep sighs communicated more than mere words. Glen managed to endure five days until he hired a car and drove his family to Lake Garda.

They were all pleased to be out of that cramped apartment and away from the ferocious summer heat of the city. Winds came down off the mountains and across the lake, making for a much more enjoyable experience. The aquamarine waters and dark green of the cypress trees along the shore were a stunning location in which to spend a few days.

In a small hotel by the lake, he and Alessandra enjoyed time lying on sun loungers while Isabella played with the other children. In a rare moment of spontaneity, Glen reached out for Alessandra's hand and squeezed it.

"Do you think I could find work here in Italy?"

"You would come live here? Oh, Glen, that would be so wonderful. Yes, I'm sure you could."

"Not too close to your mother, though."

"Definitely, wherever you want. What's changed your mind?"

"I don't know really. I suppose I'd forgotten what a wonderful country this is. La dolce vita. The food, the wine, the lifestyle."

"I'm sure Isabella would be all right for half an hour if we, you know?"

For the first time since their marriage, Glen saw only Alessandra's face and his wife felt that.

CHAPTER 13

At dinner that evening, a girl came over to their table. She looked a couple of years younger than Isabella. Glen remembered seeing them playing together that day in the hotel garden. Isabella smiled at her new friend.
"Was machst du gerade! Komm zurück!" A man grabbed the girl angrily.
"I am so sorry she disturbed you," he said in broken Italian.
"Oh, it's not a problem," began Glen but the man was already returning to his table on the far side of the room, admonishing his daughter as they went.
"Can we please go now?" said Alessandra.
"But Isabella hasn't had her ice cream yet."
"She's had quite enough for one day."
"What was that all about?" asked Glen when they were back in their room.
"German voices. I can't stand them. They did such terrible things, it makes me uncomfortable."
Glen was packing when Alessandra woke up the following morning.
"What are you doing?"

"I was thinking last night that we never had a honeymoon. I phoned the Danieli. They've had a cancellation. Isabella can stay with your mother."

Alessandra sprung out of bed and threw her arms around his neck. "I like this new romantic husband. It must be something in the water here."

The Grand Canal was just as sublime as Glen had remembered, and the palazzi had enjoyed a coat of paint since his last visit. Their room looked over the lagoon, no restricted side street view this time.

"I phoned the Ferraros and invited them for dinner here tonight," said Glen sipping the froth from his cappuccino while they took breakfast on the roof terrace surveying the lagoon and the boats going to and fro.

"That will be lovely. Without them, I wouldn't have you."

"I feel like we are masters of Venice up here. The city at our feet."

"Yes, it's a very special view."

"What would you recommend we see?" asked Glen. "You know Venice better than me."

"How about if we visit some of the islands in the lagoon. I've never been to any of them."

"Me neither. It was dark the only time I went anywhere near some of them."

Charmed by the brightly painted houses of red, saffron, pale blue, green, mauve and orange on the island of Burano, they continued onwards to Torcello. Here the mood was wistful. This location had once been a bigger centre than

Venice until plague and malaria consigned it to being a backwater. The Basilica of Santa Maria Assunta, the church of Santa Fosca, and a handful of buildings are all that remain on the flat mud expanse.

The two places of worship stand side by side. The eleventh-century church grabbed their attention with its arches and curves and terracotta tiled roof. However, appearances can be deceptive. The plain brick exterior of the basilica hides a magnificent interior of walls which glow with golden-flecked byzantine art and stunning floor mosaics. Founded in 639, it is the oldest monument in Venice.

The couple stood in awe of its beauty and inhaled the tranquility, enjoying the cool interior after the oppressive heat outside. Suddenly, Alessandra's legs collapsed beneath her like a pack of cards.

"Are you all right?" asked Glen helping her to her feet.

"Yes. Too much sun, I think."

Glen fleetingly wondered if she might be pregnant. It hadn't happened in all the years they'd been married, and he had never given it a second thought. Isabella filled his world. But if it were to happen, another child, he would like that.

"It probably is too much sun. Let's go back and get changed for dinner. I'm excited for you to meet my Italian mother and father."

The Ferraros had become rounder but their smiles were no longer painted on their faces like a Venetian mask, hiding their heartbreak. They embraced Glen warmly when they entered the lounge area on the ground floor where he and Alessandra were waiting.

"Alessandra, let me introduce you to my Italian parents."

"I'm so happy to meet you. Glen has told me about all you did for him."

"And he for us," responded Signora Ferraro.

"Let me go find a waiter. We must celebrate with a bottle of prosecco," said Glen.

Alessandra and the Ferraros sat down on the comfortable chairs amongst the pale sand colour marble columns and beneath the huge paintings adorning the walls.

"Don't we know you?" asked Signor Ferraro.

"I don't think so."

"La Pasticceria Romana. You worked there. It is you, isn't it."

"I think you must be mistaken."

Glen returned. "The waiter will be here soon."

The Ferraros exchanged a knowing glance.

"I'm so sorry, Glen. I feel a migraine coming on," said Signora Ferraro. "We were so looking forward to this evening. It has been so lovely to see you again but I really need to go. My vision is beginning to blur. Can you please excuse us."

"Of course. Maybe tomorrow, when you're feeling better-"

"Sadly these migraines last a few days when she gets them," said her husband.

"Are you upset? You look a little crestfallen," asked Alessandra as she reached out for his hand after the Ferraros had gone.

"I'm disappointed. I was very much looking forward to seeing them again, but la Signora did always suffer from bad migraines. Still, we must enjoy our last evening here."

They climbed the Campanile in Piazza San Marco to watch the sunset. At nearly one hundred metres it is the tallest building in Venice.

Hundreds of tiled roofs radiated a glow in this the golden hour. Swallows performed graceful acrobatics around the domes of St Marks to catch their supper of insects. From this height, not a single canal was visible, giving a perspective on the city they had never seen before.

"Do you love me yet, just a little?" asked Alessandra.

"I think I probably do." Glen put his arm around her shoulder.

CHAPTER 14

Glen was seated on a bench on Swanage pier. The white cliffs across the bay's cobalt waters were picture postcard perfect. Alessandra and Isabella would be back from Verona in two weeks.

"Bugger," he exclaimed when a low flying seagull left its liquid deposit on the lapel of his suit. He busied himself wiping it off with his handkerchief, oblivious to the person now standing in front of him.

"Glen?"

He raised the front of his Panama hat, which he had pulled down to keep the sun from his eyes. It was his one concession to less formal work attire during the summer months.

"Dora? I...I hadn't been expecting to see you here," said Glen getting up.

She looked a little older but no less wonderful than she'd always been.

"I came back to Swanage."

"Did you want to sit down?"

"No, my lunch break is almost over."

"How are you?"

"I'm fine now that I'm divorced."
"I didn't know you'd got married."
"It was a mistake. We weren't suited. He was very good about it. Let me divorce him on grounds of cruelty, signed papers to say that he wouldn't let me have children. Anyway, how are you and Mrs Butler?"
"We are well, thank you."
"Well, it's been nice seeing you. I really must be going."
"You too."
Glen watched her go. He wanted to call after her, but though his mouth opened no words came out. Inside he was in turmoil, his stomach churning. In Italy, he had reconciled himself to his fate and decided to embrace his situation. All was set, planned, certain. But now. But now what?
Back in the office, he couldn't concentrate. He left early. As manager since April, there was no one to tell him he couldn't. At home he couldn't relax.
Going to bed early didn't help. Agitated, he pulled on a pair of trousers and a sweater over his pyjamas and walked down the track to Chapman's Pool. A full moon lit his way. He sat in its soft light on the beach for most of the night listening to the waves running over the pebbles and thinking.
During his lunch breaks, he roamed the streets of Swanage, like a wolf stalking its prey, patient and persistent. One wet day he found her, nursing a cup of tea by a cafe window. He tapped on the glass. Her arm was vertical from her elbow, which

rested on the table. She gave an inconclusive wave. Glen took that as a yes.

"I've been looking for you," said Glen as he sat down opposite her.

"Why?"

"Because I can't get you out of mind. I thought I was over you."

"Glen, stop. Please."

"No. I've been trying to deny it these last twelve years. I can't deny it any longer. Don't tell me you don't feel the same way. I can't sleep for thinking about you."

Dora looked down at her tea as though looking for an answer, an answer that wouldn't solve anything.

"Meet me this evening. At the end of the road where your mum lives, by the postbox. I'll be there with the car at six o' clock."

He didn't wait for a reply.

She was there, waiting. He drove her out into the countryside. They got out and walked across a field and amongst the trees beyond it. As they went, they hardly spoke but they held each other's hand. The touch made their emotions boil over into a passion they couldn't control. Their love making was urgent and unrestrained down on the forest floor. An ecstasy which came from finally feeling what they had given up hope of ever experiencing.

"Tell me now that you don't feel the same way," said Glen while he caressed her hair.

"I do feel the same way, Glen. But this can't be. You

have a wife, a daughter."

"I'll tell Alessandra next week when she gets back."

"But what if she goes back to Italy and takes your daughter with her. How would you feel then? In time you'd resent me."

"She wouldn't take her. The courts wouldn't allow her to."

"I'd be breaking up a marriage."

"Like our marriage to be was broken up? I did my duty, Dora. I saved my daughter from being brought up in an orphanage. I have loved her and I will keep on loving her, always. But Alessandra and I were never meant to be. A one night fling in the confusion of war. I have tried to love her, I really have. But I have learned that love isn't something you practice like a violin so that one day it all comes together in an orchestra. It is something innate. It's either there or it's not. Not loving you, won't make me love her."

Dora didn't argue. She grabbed his head, pulling his lips towards hers.

Glen pulled back his shoulders to steel himself for what he must soon tell his wife when she and Isabella emerged out of the dense smoke which had drifted along the railway platform from the steam engine.

Isabella no longer ran to him to be spun around. She walked at her mother's side. Only thirteen and she was already assuming the dignity of her gender.

These last few months Isabella had begun the

transition from a girl to a woman. From his little Issie to a teenager who would want to find her own way. Glen mourned how quickly time had passed. She already no longer wanted to go walking each weekend or accept every chance to go on a bike ride with her father. She was growing up, growing away from him, his part in her life diminishing.

Alessandra kissed him confidently on the lips. "It's good to be home. I missed you."

"How was the journey?" asked Glen taking from her the suitcase she was carrying.

"Long, as always."

"Mama fell over on the train. And three times at Nonna's after you left. Nonna says she must see a doctor as soon as possible," blurted out Isabella.

"Don't exaggerate. I tripped."

"No, you didn't. I saw you. Your legs gave way."

"Is this true? You fell over in Venice, too. In Torcello. Remember?"

"I'll see the doctor tomorrow. I'm sure it's nothing, only dizzy spells which will pass. I'm not used to the hot Italian climate anymore."

Glen realised tonight wouldn't be the best time to tell her about Dora coming back into his life. He would wait a couple of days. He had waited all these years. A few days would make no difference. He fervently hoped Alessandra wasn't pregnant. Would he be trapped again like before?

A couple of days became a few weeks when the doctor wanted her to see a consultant at Poole hospital.

"Multiple sclerosis? How can they be sure?" asked Glen after Isabella had gone upstairs to bed.

"They say that I have all the symptoms, numbness, temporary loss of vision, the falls."

"But you never mentioned anything."

"I didn't want to worry you. When the numbness and aches first started a few months ago, I didn't want to say anything. We had our holiday all planned, and when we were there, we were having such a lovely time. I thought I could escape my past but I can't. This illness is God's judgment on me."

"Don't be silly. It's no such thing."

"That's because you don't know the real Alessandra Faccini."

CHAPTER 15

1943

While she sat on a bench inside Santa Lucia station waiting for morning to arrive, Alessandra replayed the conversation in her mind.

"Signor Rizzo came to visit me today," said her mother while she served dinner.

"Whatever for?"

"You know his poor wife died last year."

"Yes, but what does that have to do with anything?"

"He's lonely, and has three children to care for. It's hard for him. He has that bakery to run. He was very complimentary about your work."

"Well, he could pay me more than the pittance he does if that's what he really thinks."

"In your father's absence, he wanted to ask my permission to court you."

"To court me? Absolutely not. He's at least twenty years older than me, and he smells worse than the River Adige on a hot August day."

"Alessandra, look at us. Look at this meal. Pasta with a few drops of olive oil. When could we last afford meat or anything nice? Since they sent your father to Germany, we haven't received a single lira. Marry Signor Rizzo and you'll never be hungry again."

"I can't marry a man for hunger. A man I don't love and would never love."

"Love. Huh! We women cannot marry for love. Love doesn't provide a roof over our heads. We marry so that we are no longer a burden on our parents. If you don't accept his offer, you'll probably lose your job, and then where will you be? Answer me that. You need to come down from the clouds. Refuse him and I can't keep you."

"I'm not asking you to. I'll go to Venice and get a job there."

"What nonsense. You'll end up working in a brothel to survive."

"No Signorina, we have no vacancies," repeated at each restaurant or shop Alessandra entered became the recurring refrain of her first day in the city.

Shortly before the evening curfew began, she found a room in a small pensione in the Cannaregio district on the Fondamenta della Sensa in northern Venice.

Only a few lira remained in her purse. Alessandra fretted what would become of her if tomorrow she found no employment. The curfew meant sleeping outside would be too risky. She would need to leave town, walk across the bridge to the mainland and keep walking until she found a field to sleep in.

Not expecting success, her first call next morning was La Pasticceria Romana only two doors down from the pensione.

"Can you make cakes and decorate them?" asked the rather doleful looking proprietor. His shoulders were hunched as he shuffled around, shooing away the pigeons and wiping the outside tables which overlooked the canal.

"Yes. I worked in a pasticceria in Verona."

"Well, you can benefit from my misfortune. The fascists took my son last month to go and fight for them. It is too much work for me without him. I'll try you for a week. You can lodge in his old room on the second floor. My name is Giorgio Lamberti. Follow me."

Signor Lamberti led her up the rickety stairs and into a small room. He opened the shutters. Dust particles danced in the bright light like tiny stars of welcome.

There was a bed, a wooden chair, and a cupboard

"It's not much I'm afraid."

"It's perfect, and what a view," said Alessandra as she stuck her head out of the window.

She could see right along the canal. It was wider than most in the city. On the opposite side, there was no pavement, only the faded paint and exposed plaster of the buildings directly abutting onto the water.

"That's out of bounds," said Signor Lamberti, noticing her look at the steep ladder-like stairs leading to the attic when they went to go downstairs. "I keep my son's things in there, for his return."

Signor Lamberti wasn't a bad boss just a gloomy one who frequently hit the bottle. Alessandra made no judgment. His wife had died last year, and now his second son was gone. Their first had been captured on the Russian front. Everyone knew that prisoners in Russia were unlikely to survive.

The shop reflected his lack of attention. Alessandra threw herself into her new job with gusto. She spring cleaned the cafe until it sparkled. The weeks passed. She had to work from morning until night but she didn't mind. At least she wouldn't be marrying a man old enough to be her father.

Supplies were erratic so some days there were no pastries to make, and even on the best days the display cabinet was never anywhere near full. Although that didn't matter a great deal since few Venetians had the spare cash any longer to treat themselves. Most of the time they struggled to pay for the basics, but that didn't stop them coming in for a coffee to talk with their neighbours.

"Buongiorno."

Alessandra looked up from rearranging the few fresh cakes which she was setting out in such a way to convey the impression that there were more than they had. The chatter of locals standing drinking their espressos at the marble counter halted.

A German officer stood before her in his grey

uniform, his face partially obscured by his peaked cap while he looked down at the counter.

"I'll have a coffee. Bring it to me, I'll be sitting outside. And one of those cakes too. That one with fruit on the top." He jabbed his finger against the glass in the manner of a man used to giving commands which others obeyed without question.

He spoke Italian with a distinct German accent. He turned and went outside. Alessandra watched him while he went. A black belt high on his waist, his gun in a holster on his right-hand side. Black boots came almost to his knees. The overall effect was oppressive and intimidating as if he were a servant of Satan.

Sitting outside in the bright sunshine, he became more human. He removed his cap, revealing hair the colour of straw. Bella, Signor Lamberti's cat, jumped onto his lap and he began stroking her. He couldn't be all bad, thought Alessandra. That feline rarely took to a man.

He smiled at Alessandra when she placed his order on the table. His blue eyes seemed exotic to her, unaccustomed as she was to seeing eyes of that colour. Alessandra scurried back inside, scolding herself that her heart should be beating faster. Not wanting to, but unable to resist the urge, she found herself looking outside at regular intervals. He was undeniably handsome, possessing a strong jaw and perfect bone structure.

Finishing his coffee, he came in to pay.

"You've given me too much."

"That doesn't matter, keep it as a tip."

He returned every few days, taking coffee and a cake at an outside table on each occasion. No one else sat outside when he was there. Like being in the vicinity of an alpha male lion which would growl aggressively if approached, others kept their distance. Alessandra responded to his questions for her name and where she was from. He told her his name was Gunther Schulte and that he was from Ulm in southern Germany. His family owned a printing company there which he would take over from his father when the war ended.

"Do you like the opera, Alessandra?" he asked one morning while she served him.

"I've never been. Though on summer evenings I would occasionally hang about near the Arena in Verona to listen to it."

"Then you must come with me to La Fenice tomorrow night. They're performing Puccini's 'Madame Butterfly'."

"I can't."

"Why can't you? I'll meet you in front at six o'clock. Be there or I'll have you sent back to Verona." He laughed as though joking but the laugh sounded insincere.

Alessandra was late. She almost hadn't gone.

"You look prettier than a sunset," said Schulte, bowing formally and kissing her hand. "We should hurry, it's about to start."

Alessandra was uncomfortable being in such close

proximity to so many Nazis and supporters of the Italian Social Republic. Such thoughts were briefly forgotten while Schulte led her up the grand staircase and into a private box of red velvet chairs and plush curtains. The space was gilded with gold lamps and gold edged mirrors.

Leaning forwards in her seat, she marvelled at the lavishness of the venue. It curved in a three-quarter circle five stories high above the main seating area. A massive chandelier hung down from the pale blue ceiling where a fresco of heavenly figures flew.

She imagined herself a diva, performing in this great venue as flowers were thrown at her in appreciation. Her reverie was interrupted by trumpets playing the opening strains of Giovinezza, or Youth, the Italian fascist anthem.

Alessandra had no option but to stand and sing like everybody else. Germans could be excused for not knowing the words but not an Italian. Although looking straight ahead, she could sense Schulte observing her, checking her loyalty to the cause. When the anthem ended, Italians and Germans alike raised their right arms in salute. She was obliged to do the same.

Alessandra's thoughts of betrayal faded once the curtain rose. She fought to control her emotions while the arias were sung. Her tears flowed freely when Butterfly killed herself and her erstwhile lover rushed in too late to save her.

Schulte passed her his handkerchief as the stage

curtains fell and the audience rose to give a standing ovation.

"Wasn't that beautiful, Alessandra?"

"Beyond beautiful."

"We should come again. Come, I have transport to take you home."

CHAPTER 16

Schulte led her to a motorboat waiting in the canal outside and gave a brusque order in German. They slipped out into the Grand Canal and Schulte moved closer to her on the bench on which they were seated. Alessandra looked away, pretending to admire the passing palazzi, which were invisible in the darkness. He put his hands on her face and turned her towards him. His hands were strong and determined.

His lips connected with hers. She knew that she should resist but he had an animal magnetism that drew her in, a powerful force like a lead weight which would pull her to the bottom of the canal and hold her there no matter how hard she kicked.

"Meet me at La Fenice, same time and same day next week," he said when he helped her disembark. Alessandra feared what she might well be getting into but she didn't want to fight it, the feelings which he had awakened in her were too thrilling to forgo.

While Alessandra climbed the stairs to her room,

she heard footsteps above her and a door shutting. It couldn't be Signor Lamberti. She'd already passed his room on the first floor and heard him snoring.

Reaching her floor, she saw the door opposite her room was open, as was her own. The sound of a closing door could only have come from the attic. The place where she had been forbidden to go. She wondered who could live there, and why they needed to hide. A young man perhaps, not wanting to be sent off to fight. She would do the same in his position. Why should anyone have to risk their life for a cause which they didn't believe in, a cause that egotistical maniacs had created for their own aggrandisement, not caring about the dehumanising effect on those they ruled with an iron fist.

"You were out late last night, Alessandra," said Signor Lamberti while he arranged the chairs around the three circular indoor tables while they prepared to open the next morning.

"I went to visit an old friend from Verona. She works in San Polo. We hadn't seen each other for so long that we talked and talked and forgot how late it was."

"I was thinking of going to visit my wife's mother in Vicenza tomorrow for a week. Do you think you could manage on your own while I was gone?"

"Of course I could, Signor Lamberti."

"Then I shall go. I'm pleased you came here. You're a hard worker."

Each time she climbed the stairs, Alessandra looked up at the attic door, but she never saw it open or heard any further noise. Maybe it had all been in her imagination, she told herself.

Schulte didn't come the next day or the next, but in the afternoon of that day a German soldier arrived. "SS-Gruppen Führer Schulte has sent me to deliver this poster. You are to put it on the wall in recognition of the friendship between our two great countries. Take it."

Alessandra unfurled it. The poster read *La Germania e veramente vostra amica (Germany is truly your friend)*. It pictured a helmeted German soldier, his right hand outstretched in greeting. A rifle protruded above his left shoulder, a reminder that refusal to accept the hand of friendship wasn't an option.

"Heil Hitler." The soldier saluted and left.

A nail protruded from the wall behind the counter. Alessandra put the poster there, pushing the top of it against the nail until it broke the paper.

That night she lay in bed wondering why Schulte hadn't been today. She had to admit to herself that she was disappointed. He'd been so attentive at the opera, but that poster was hardly romantic. Signor Lamberti would hate it. Yet she couldn't take it down, Schulte might come to check she'd put it up.

A few days later while getting into bed, she heard a sound coming from downstairs in the cafe.

Alessandra pulled the sheet over her head. She wasn't going to go down alone to investigate.

Anyway, it was probably just paranoia. A mouse or a rat, that must be it. She must stop feeding Bella. Signor Lamberti would chide her whenever she did.

"That cat will never catch vermin if you keep filling her belly," he'd told her.

But no, wait… there was someone. She heard a creak on the floorboards outside her room. Then another.

She climbed out of bed and picked up the wooden chair and stood against the wall by the door. If the intruder came in, she would hit him on the head and make a run for it.

Alessandra stood there for several minutes yet no one tried to enter. It can't have been anyone, she reassured herself. Only my mind playing tricks. Probably…

She angled the chair under the door handle. That would keep any assailant out, and if not give her warning so that she could jump out of bed and assault him with the chair.

Or was it perhaps the person who lived in the attic? Had he gone downstairs for food with Signor Lamberti absent, no longer able to feed him? Though even that thought didn't help her sleep.

Mid afternoon the following day, Alessandra put up the closed sign. She only needed a short nap, but she did need one. She didn't want to look exhausted for Gunther. Tonight she would be meeting him again at La Fenice.

Moreover, a box had arrived that morning, tied

with a yellow ribbon. The regular customers looked on agog, eager for her to open it there and then. A secret admirer, one commented, as the others waited eagerly for her answer. Alessandra's cheeks turned pink with embarrassment.

"Probably from my Nonna. She always gets the date of my birthday wrong," she lied.

She'd put the box on the shelf behind her, but all morning it had prayed on her mind. Now alone in her room, she lay the box on the bed. Tissue paper rustled as she unwrapped the gift inside. It was a red silk dress, and there was a note:

I saw this and thought of you x

A frisson of happiness rushed through her. Alessandra had never owned a dress this beautiful. She took off her plain work dress marked with coffee stains and put it on. She beamed when she looked at herself in the mirror on the wall.

She imagined herself wearing it and going to a ball on the arm of her prince charming. It was Gunther's face that she saw.

A noise from upstairs interrupted her daydreaming. She looked up as she opened her bedroom door. Two small, wan faces peeped out from the attic door which was slightly ajar, one above the other, like two peas in a pod. One a boy, the other a girl, brother and sister, twins by the look of them.

Alessandra smiled. They didn't smile back. Their eyes showed no curiosity, only fear that they had been seen.

"Hello, I'm Alessandra."

They shut the door. Alessandra went downstairs and picked two cakes with chocolate and a strawberry on top. Going back up, she left them on the top step outside the attic door. They had disappeared when she left early that evening.

CHAPTER 17

Alessandra agreed to dine with Gunther after the opera. He took her back to the Gritti Palace Hotel where he lived. He had a suite overlooking the Grand Canal.

They were served in his room. Alessandra had never experienced such a glamorous lifestyle. The furnishings were exquisite, all period pieces of quality. Such a far cry from her humble life. From the balcony, she could see the perfect architectural lines of Santa Maria della Salute set against scudding night clouds, the moon casting a ghostly light upon them.

After dinner, she didn't resist his advances. She didn't want to.

"Gunther," she said while they lay in his bed.

"Yes."

"My father was sent to Germany to work. I worry what has become of him. Could you help me find out?"

Before answering, Gunther lit a cigarette and inhaled. He blew out a ring of smoke in a display of dominance. "I may be able to."

"What in God's name is that?" said Signor Lamberti glaring at the poster when he returned from Vicenza. "Did you put that up there?"

"I had no choice. A German soldier arrived with it and told me we had to display it."

"Be careful, Alessandra. I saw Max as I walked back here. He told me that a fancy box arrived for you the other day. This poster is a lie. The Germans are not our friends, no matter how good looking or charming some of them might seem."

She wanted to ask him about the children who lived in his attic and why but now didn't seem the right time.

Alessandra ignored his advice and accepted Schulte's invitation to dinner in his hotel room a few days later.

"I have news about your father."

"You do?"

This could be wonderful news. She missed him terribly, and her mother would be so happy to know he was still alive when she told her.

"He's working in a munitions factory in Hamburg. I'm worried for him. It is dangerous work. The British and Americans are bombing the city daily. He sleeps in the factory."

"Can you not get him out? You must be high up in the army to live here."

"I wish it were so easy. You know if I could, I would do it gladly. But I need to offer those in charge something in return. I need your help."

"My help?"

"Yes, your help. You see, my instructions are to round up all Jews and send them to Poland. The Führer has decided the best thing for them is to move them there so they can all live together, in one place. That way, they can live as they want. If you had information that could help find any Jews, it would be enough to get your father released and brought home to Italy. We believe many are hiding in the city. You talk to people all day long and listen to their conversations. You must hear things."

Without thinking, Alessandra placed a hand across her mouth.

"You know something, don't you."

"Are you certain such people would come to no harm?"

"None whatsoever. They would be re-united with their own kind. Many Jewish families have become separated. Some have already gone leaving behind loved ones. I have even heard of children left here in Venice. Their parents in Poland are worried sick about them."

"If I were to hear anything, what would happen to those who have hidden them?"

"They would have broken the law. But if they were friends of yours, I could make an exception. Think carefully, Alessandra. Every day your father stays where he is, he risks death. He needs your help, and soon. Don't gamble with his life."

The customers in La Pasticceria Romana turned around, their eyes wide with fear when they heard the loud, ugly march of boots invade the cafe the next morning. Schulte barked orders in German. The four men with him clattered noisily up the stairs, kicking open doors and upending furniture. Signor Lamberti looked at Alessandra, his eyes penetrating and accusing. She turned away in shame.

A couple of minutes later the soldiers returned, two of them carrying the children. They didn't utter a word but it was evident that they were terrified.

"You will come with us," said Schulte pointing at Signor Lamberti.

Signor Lamberti came from behind the counter.

"Go," demanded Schulte pushing him in the back with his pistol.

The captives were marched along the Fondamenta. Two soldiers were out in front, behind them the two children walking side by side, holding hands and heads bowed. There followed the two other soldiers, then Signor Lamberti with Schulte at the rear.

Alessandra came running after him. "Where are you taking him? You promised."

"Come to my room this evening," he said without looking at her.

Venetians watched from their doorways. Women made the sign of the cross over their chests as the group passed.

The customers stared at Alessandra when she returned. Each left without saying a word, but their frowns pronounced her guilt. No more customers came that day.

More jurors watched and concurred with their verdict when she made her way along the path by the canal at dusk.

Alessandra flung open the door to Schulte's suite.

"What have you done with Signor Lamberti?"

"He is being interrogated. We need to find out what else he has been up to and make sure that he isn't part of the resistance."

"And then you'll let him go?"

"If he's innocent. That decision isn't mine to make."

"And the children?"

"They are on their way. It seems their parents are already in Poland. You should be pleased. They will be reunited with them."

"Have you made arrangements for my father to be sent home?"

"I have indeed. I sent a message as soon as I got back. It may be some days until they can find a seat on a train across Germany and through the Alps. Don't be impatient. Now stop pacing up and down and come here."

Schulte grabbed her arm.

"Let go of me!"

He didn't. He pulled her to him and slapped her hard across the face. Then he threw her back on the bed. She knew better than to retaliate. How could she fight when she was guilty, when she loathed the person who she had become.

Signor Lamberti was executed. His body hung on

hastily erected scaffolding in front of the Madonna dell'Orto, a short walk from the pasticceria, along with four others accused of being partisans.

They hung there for three days as a warning to others. Stone saints perched high on the warm, red brickwork of the church looked down upon the macabre display. Alessandra didn't see it but a former customer came in to tell her. He spat at her before leaving.

The authorities confiscated the business and the building. A family loyal to il Duce, Mussolini, were moved in. Alessandra was required to sleep in the attic. She cried when she found a doll under the bed.

Schulte ordered Alessandra to remain at the pasticceria and keep working as normal. German soldiers and Italian fascists became her new customers. The locals boycotted the place.

Now a photograph of Mussolini hung with Hitler's on the wall. Some nights the front window was smashed but it seemed no one dared harm Alessandra.

She wanted to return to Verona and wait there for her father but Schulte forbade it. They still attended the opera regularly, although Alessandra now dreaded going. To her, La Fenice had become a monstrous caricature of itself, a purgatory where she was now condemned to sit with the devil's foot soldiers. The worst to endure were the operas of Wagner. All day long her ears were already assaulted by the harsh sounds of the German language at the cafe. Rarely did she get to hear 'la bella lingua' any longer. She'd been buried alive in a coffin of Teutonic cacophony.

Repeated requests about her father were rebuffed by demands she be patient. Trains were needed to bring soldiers and supplies, Schulte claimed. Finally, one day Schulte told her that he'd received news her father had been killed in an air raid.

Alessandra realised too late that his promise to find him and bring him home had most probably always been a lie. Her naivety had cost three innocent lives.

Some mornings, Alessandra struggled to get out of bed. Hope had flown long ago. She sank deeper into the morass of betrayal her life had become.

If the Germans lost the war, where could she go? She was a traitor. If they stayed, she would have to keep on doing what she hated, serving them and being Schulte's whore. She was living in despair and she would go to hell when she died.

In late February 1945, Schulte sent her a message. He had been recalled to Germany. It was goodbye and good luck.

Then one day at the end of April, the Germans began pulling out. Alessandra thought briefly of running after them and seeking a ride out. But she didn't care enough anymore to try and save herself. She would accept her fate.

CHAPTER 18

1958

"So now you know why I deserve this disease. It's divine retribution."

"You shouldn't think like that, Alessandra," said Glen.

"Tell me then that you don't think less of me for what I did."

"It was a war. Terrible things happened, no one was blameless. Anyway, you didn't do anything with bad intent. Schulte made you believe the children would be taken care of, and that no harm would come to Signor Lamberti. You did what you did to save your father, not appreciating others would suffer as a consequence."

"It's kind of you to say so, but how could I have been so gullible? I should have listened to Signor Lamberti, taken his advice. I was reckless."

Alessandra's legs gave way and she fell to the floor. Glen helped her to the sofa. They both sat in solemn silence.

Although he fought not to show it, Glen was shaken by her revelation. With the benefit of hindsight, it was obvious what a terrible mistake she'd made. But there was nothing to be gained by saying any more about it. She was slowly dying. She would never get to see their daughter marry or meet her grandchildren. If she believed she deserved to be punished, that was surely punishment enough.

"Don't dwell on the past. We can't change it. You should enjoy your time with Isabella."

Alessandra touched his hand. "I will, and you should be with the woman you love."

Glen's mouth dropped open. "How do you know about her?"

"It was obvious from the moment I got back from Italy. The way you were when I kissed you at the station. I could sense it immediately. It's all right, Glen. I'm not angry. Is she the one you left so you could marry me?"

"Yes, Dora's her name. We were to be married, then your letter came."

"I'm sorry. I won't be a burden to you any longer. I shall go back to Verona. Mama will take care of me. I should like to take Isabella. It shouldn't be for many months. The consultant says it's progressing rapidly. I know you'll miss her but grant me this one wish. I'll send her back before I become totally dependent on others."

"No, we'll manage, somehow. We shouldn't interrupt her schooling. She has all her friends here."

"All right, but I will need assistance before long.

What does Dora do? It would be nice for her to get to know Isabella."

"I don't think we should tell her about me and Dora. She might feel rejected. It can come out over time. Once…"

"Once I'm gone you mean. If that's what you want. But I would still like to meet the woman who captured your heart, and if she could be around naturally, helping me, it might ease the transition for our daughter."

Dora came to visit a few days later. Glen brought her while Isabella was at school.

"This is Dora. I'll give you a few minutes to get acquainted while I put the kettle on."

Dora stood defensively, holding her handbag in front of her skirt as if to shield herself.

"Men," laughed Alessandra. "They find it so awkward to talk about relationships. Do sit down. I am so pleased to meet you, Dora. I don't resent you. I want Glen to be happy. He gave up so many years for us when he could have been with you. It helps to know that he will finally have what he wants. He saved my life, in more ways than one."

"I'm sorry, I never wanted to wreck your marriage."

"There was nothing to wreck. And didn't I do the same to yours? Poetic justice, as you English say. I no longer need feel guilty for keeping Glen from you. At last, we can all be free of guilt. Glen says you may be able to come during the week to help me. I'm afraid that I am falling over and dropping things more often every day."

"Yes, I only work mornings. I could be here from one o'clock."

"That would be perfect, and you will get to know Isabella. She normally gets home from school by half past four. I'm glad to know she will still have a woman to help guide her and confide in when I am no longer here. Glen is a devoted father, but girls do need a mother figure in their life."

"Oh, I could never replace you."

"I'm not worried about that. Isabella's heart is big enough to love all of us."

Alessandra's health deteriorated quickly. By early November, she was confined to a wheelchair.

Glen put a bed in the lounge for her. He dressed her before leaving for work and sat her in her chair. Dora came as agreed. It didn't feel wrong anymore to sneak a kiss, or more, when he drove her home after he got back from work.

Yet Glen's happiness wasn't complete. It hurt to see Alessandra suffer and lose her independence. Though he didn't love her, he was extremely fond of her. She had given him the greatest gift of all, their wonderful daughter.

And Isabella, what must she be feeling? She'd assured him she was fine but he heard her crying when he passed her door at night. Once he entered her room to comfort her but she told him she needed to be alone.

Isabella was fourteen now. There was much he couldn't give her. Alessandra had been wise to invite Dora into their home. She and Isabella were developing a bond, a level of trust that would help her when Alessandra died.

The doctor told Glen he'd never seen a case progress so fast. Glen suspected she willed it to be that way. She could no longer fight her demons.

One evening, while he sat with Alessandra watching the dancing flames in the fireplace and enjoying the heat on his feet pushed out towards it, she surprised him.

"Take me to Venice, will you? One last time."

"Do you think you're fit to travel?"

"I'll never be as fit again as I am today. It's now or never, Glen. I want to go and lay some flowers for those I betrayed."

Glen didn't challenge her. She rarely asked for anything. He could see from her expression that this was important to her. He couldn't deny her, it might help ease the pain of her past.

By the following week, it had all been arranged. Dora would stay at the house to keep an eye on Isabella. Alessandra sat in her wheelchair in the hallway looking out for their taxi.

"Everything will be fine. Don't worry Glen," said Dora.

"Give me a kiss then, a proper one."

They didn't see Isabella come into the kitchen and quickly leave, running back upstairs. They were too caught up in each other's passionate embrace.

Glen was glum, something which he'd never experienced before when he had stayed at the Danieli. The luxury of it didn't thrill him this time. The morning view when he flung back the curtains to a day of late November sunshine failed to raise his spirits.

Alessandra touched his head gently while he kneeled on the floor to put on her shoes.

"Glen, I have one last favour to ask. Tonight when we return, I need your help. Can you fill the bath, I mean really fill it. Not just a few centimetres. Help me in and then go downstairs for a drink and leave me in peace."

Glen got up and sat down in the chair opposite her. "Think about what you're saying, Alessandra. You're asking me to help you commit suicide. I'd be committing a serious crime."

"I don't want to go on, Glen. I've read about what comes next. I'll be a vegetable. Become incontinent. Die a horrible death, choking when I can no longer swallow. I don't want to die like that, without any dignity. I don't want you or Isabella to see me in that state. No one will blame you. All they will know is that I drowned in the bath."

"I can't do it. I can't. I'm sorry but I can't help you kill yourself. I wish you didn't have to suffer like this but it won't be long now. I'll speak to the doctor when we get back. Get you into hospital. I'm sure they can sedate you with morphine or something so you won't know what's going on."

Glen got up from his chair. "We should go."

She looked at her husband, imploring him with her eyes.

"It's no good, Alessandra. I can't do this last thing

you ask of me. It's a step too far. We need to leave now but first I'm going to put some plastic covers over your shoes. Acqua alta is in an hour."

Glen put some on his shoes too. They covered their calves also. Water had already begun to bubble up like a spring from under the paving in several places when they passed through St. Mark's Square.

November was a notorious time for high water. City workers had laid narrow wooden boards on metal legs in long lines to create a walkway for those unprepared. But there was a subliminal beauty to acqua alta. It transformed the Piazza into a shallow lake, the water reflecting its magnificent buildings.

At times the floods could be serious, as in November 1966, when the city was submerged under nearly two metres of water and great damage was done. Today, it was less than thirty centimetres at its deepest.

Suitably attired, they were able to thread their way through the streets towards the sestiere of Cannaregio, not having to turn back like those who weren't and didn't want to spend a day with wet feet and soggy trousers. The raised wooden boards were only put out in Piazza San Marco.

While he pushed his wife, Glen realised he had never noticed how wheelchair unfriendly the city was. Many of the bridges over the canals, though not that high, had steps to surmount. But why would he have noticed? He'd never expected to be pushing one.

CHAPTER 19

Morning sun surrendered to grey clouds.They stopped at a florist. Alessandra chose two bunches of flowers. Glen laid them on her lap. They went first to the Ghetto.

Deriving from the Venetian word getto, meaning foundry, it lost that purpose in the early sixteenth century when the city's Jews were forced to live there, sealed in by gates at night and cut off by wide canals. Outside walls were windowless to add to their isolation from the rest of the city. Restricted in space and limited in how high they could build, the population kept their ceilings low in height to fit in as many floors as possible, giving the impression of a Hobbit's medieval Manhattan.

The place bore a forlorn appearance in the November drizzle. The trees in the square were bare and skeletal. It seemed fitting for the purpose of their visit.

Stopping in front of the memorial, Glen placed flowers at its foot and stood back. Alessandra had her head bowed and was whispering, her fingers interlocked, the finger tips resting on her knuckles. She was praying, as she had for years, that the boy and girl had survived the concentration camps. It was a possibility, though an unlikely one, and one the answer to which she would never know.

When she raised her head, she nodded and he pushed her the short distance to their next destination.

The pasticceria was no longer there. A restaurant, closed and shuttered that day, had taken its place. Glen laid the other bunch of flowers for her. A tear ran down Alessandra's face which Glen gently wiped away with his hand.

"Come on, let's go."

They stopped in a restaurant to eat lunch. Glen ordered them gnocchi. Other pasta could be difficult to feed her, especially spaghetti or tagliatelle. Glen wanted to shout at the other diners who stared at them. Get on with your meals, she's not a freak show.

For desert, he ordered tiramisu. It was her favourite and she hadn't eaten any since they were here in August when life had seemed so promising and so uncomplicated.

Weary from pushing her wheelchair, Glen was glad when he saw the lagoon at the end of Calle delle Rasse. The entrance to the Danieli was just around the corner.

Up in their room, he fell fast asleep on the bed. When he awoke, it was already getting dark. He went to put on the lights.

"I'm sorry for leaving you sitting in the dark like that. I feel refreshed now. Is there anything else you want to do? We have to go straight to the airport in the morning."

"There is one thing. Could you take me to confession in San Marco?"

"Didn't you already confess everything to the priest back home?"

"I want to do it here where it all happened."

Unlike most cathedrals in western Europe, St. Mark's is byzantine in both design and decoration. It would have looked at home much further east. But then Venice had embraced so much from Asia. The city had grown rich and powerful by controlling the trade in goods from that continent, until Vasco da Gama of Portugal found a way around Africa to India at the end of the fifteenth century. That discovery had broken la Serenissima's monopoly and marked the start of her decline.

Candles gave a deeply atmospheric lighting as they entered the cathedral. Glen pushed Alessandra into a confessional and went to sit in the central area. He gazed up at its stupendous curved and domed ceilings of gold and hovering apostles.

Religion had never brought him any comfort but he hoped it would for Alessandra. Although if the nuns from his orphanage were to be believed, she would be heading for a long spell in purgatory, if not eternal damnation in hell itself.

He was still looking upwards at the ceiling when

a cough attracted his attention. The priest had pushed Alessandra back to him. He gave Glen a look of compassion.

"We should head back to the hotel for dinner," said Glen.

"Can we eat in the room tonight. I'm really not hungry. Order for yourself and I can have a couple of mouthfuls. I won't want any more."

Glen would rather have eaten in the restaurant with other people. Sitting together in their room was funereal, like a last supper. Once they got home, it wouldn't be long until it was all over. He could sense the will to live fast seeping out of her. A leak had become an unstoppable flow.

"Shall I get you ready for bed?"

"Can we go out and wander through a few back streets and take in the atmosphere one last time?"

"Do we have to?"

"Please, it's my last chance."

Glen pushed her through Piazza San Marco. The tourists had retreated to warm bars and restaurants. Only the occasional solitary figure crossed the square, collar up and head down against the cold. It was quiet and brooding.

Glen was glad he'd agreed to come out. Never had he had the centre of Venetian tourism all to himself like this. Before the advent of mass travel, the city's iconic sights must have been like this most nights, not only late on a damp November evening.

They turned right out of the square near St

Mark's cathedral and disappeared into the maze of alleys and waterways. The shadows were long, the lighting sparse.

"Stop," said Alessandra. "There's something I need to tell you."

They were by a canal in a back street. It was deserted, almost eerily so.

"What now?" Glenn couldn't hide his irritation. It had been a long and tiring day.

"Come round in front of me so I can see you."

Glen complied.

"I went to confession today to confess something I have never told you. Something I've hidden from you all these years. I lied about Isabella's date of birth. The birth certificate which you have seen is a forgery. She was born in 1945."

It was as though a hand grenade had exploded inside of him. For a moment, Glen was too stunned to speak while he tried to absorb what she had told him.

"What do you mean? Are you saying she's not mine? She has my nose, my smile. You always tell me that."

"I said those things so you would believe it, believe that she was yours."

Glen spun around and walked away a few steps before coming back. He leaned forwards until his face was only inches from hers, the vein in his forehead pulsating with growing rage.

"How could you do this?"

"I couldn't leave her in the orphanage, and I

couldn't let her know she had a monster for a father. Anyway, you're not completely blameless. You were happy to take me, not caring whether you made me pregnant or not."

"But she wasn't mine. You knew she wasn't mine. You stole my life. Dora and I could have had children of our own. What kind of person are you!" In anger, he pushed at the arms of her wheelchair. It rolled slowly but inexorably back towards the canal.

Glen could have run forward to grab the wheelchair. Instead, he chose to let it go. The rear wheels cleared the edge of the paving stones and as they did so the wheelchair began to assume a steep downwards angle.

Glen saw the look on Alessandra's face. There was no fear, no cries for help. She looked calm. Satisfied. Her wish granted.

Water sloshed against the edges of the canal a few times. Then all became perfectly still again. There was nothing to see, only a viscous blackness and a thin crescent moon reflected in the water.

CHAPTER 20

Glen was seated alone in a police cell reliving the last few hours.

Sprinting from the canal, he burst into a nearby bar like a feral beast, wild eyed and incoherent. The barman had to ask him to repeat what he said. The man called the police and sat Glen down with a coffee, observing his shaking hands when he raised the cup to his lips.

Two policemen arrived and asked Glen to show them where. Curious customers left the bar and followed behind them. They would have something new to gossip about for days.

Glen pointed at the spot.

"There's nothing we can do until morning. You must come with us to give a statement."

"Let me check that I've got this right," said the interrogating officer to Glen in the interview room. "Your wife was confined to a wheelchair. She wanted you to take her out on a cold night through dark alleys. She asked you to stop by the side of a canal. You turned away for a moment. When you turned around, she had moved the wheels

backwards and was already falling into the canal."
"Yes. She wanted to die. When we arrived yesterday, she asked me to fill the bath and leave her alone so she could drown herself. I refused."
"Hmm. That's your story?"
"It's not a story."
"We're going to have to hold you overnight."
"I want to see a lawyer."
"In Italy you have no right to. I can ask someone from the British Consulate to come and see you if you would like."

There were no windows in his cell and no clock, but Glen was convinced it must already be light. Divers would be going down to locate her body and bring her out, wet and lifeless.

How could this have happened? Was what she'd told him true? Had she only said all that to make him angry, hoping he would do something rash exactly like he had?

Though why would she have been so cruel to say such a thing if it wasn't the truth? Isabella's eyes were brown, her hair was brown. So were his. But what did that prove? Schulte's eyes and hair could have been that colour. Or he could have been Hitler's perfect Aryan specimen, blond and blue-eyed, yet with an Italian mother, hair and eye colour would have been a complete lottery.

Keys turned in the lock. He was escorted to another room. It looked similar to where he'd been interrogated. A man in a double breasted suit and handkerchief poking out of his top pocket got up to greet him.

"Good morning Mr Butler. I'm Gerrard Ballingall, the British Vice Consul. I understand you're in a spot of bother."

"That's one way of putting it. I need a lawyer."

"They won't give you one, yet."

"Well, when then?"

"They can hold you for up to three days before bringing you before the magistrates who will appoint a lawyer. That is if the police charge you."

"And if they do?"

"If the charge is murder, you would be remanded until trial. They can hold you for up to three years without a trial."

"Three years! You've got to be joking."

"The wheels of Italian justice do turn painfully slowly but I'm sure it will be quicker than that. I'm afraid they may charge you to give themselves time to gather evidence. You're a Johnny foreigner here. If they let you return to England, they'd have to get you back. It's easier for them to complete their investigations before releasing you. I'm sorry to be the bearer of bad tidings but that's the way things work here. Is there anyone you'd like me to let know that you're here?"

Glen thought of Isabella. He wanted to be the one to tell her. He would count on being freed soon. "No, not at the moment, thank you."

"I'll keep in touch with the authorities, and visit you again if things don't go as you hope. Good luck, Mr Butler."

Two days later, Glen was led into a wood-panelled court room to stand before the magistrates who sat on their dais in a palazzo by the Rialto bridge. The words *Legge e Uguale per Tutti* (*All are equal before the law)* were carved in the mahogany above them. Glen declined their offer of a translator and pleaded not guilty to murder.

Later that day, an enclosed boat took him and other prisoners out to Giudecca, the long spine-like island lying south of the city and then an industrial suburb, a scruffy place of decay but one which offered a magnificent view of Venice for those at liberty to walk its promenade. Derived from giudicati, judged, and a place of banishment for troublesome nobles many centuries ago, Giudecca's prison was to be Glen's new home.

CHAPTER 21

She stood there in the doorway. Black hat, black coat, like the grim reaper. Isabella knew the answer to her question before she asked it.

"Mama?"

The woman nodded and held out her arms for her granddaughter. She felt Isabella's convulsions against her chest. That bastard must pay for this, the old woman swore to herself.

"Where's Papa?"

"Let's go sit down, my dear."

Isabella led her to the sitting room. Her grandmother sat next to her on the sofa and took her hands in hers.

"Your Papa has been arrested."

Isabella drew back in horror and disbelief.

"He pushed your mother into a canal, in her wheelchair." Signora Faccini choked on a sob. "I have come to bring you home, take you back to Verona with me."

"It can't be true," said Isabella. "It can't."

Then she thought of him and Dora, the repulsive kissing she'd witnessed. Her poor mother.

Betrayed by her father. Betrayed while she was helpless and dying.

Isabella didn't remember much of the next hour or even the journey to Verona. She didn't question her Nonna. She was the only branch of certainty which she could cling to as life threw her down the rapids.

Her mother was gone. As for her father, she could never forgive him, even if she wanted to. He'd been having an affair with her mother's carer behind her back. Should he be found not guilty of killing her mother, she would still hate him. He disgusted her.

Glen's prison was near the Zitelle church, sinner next to saint. He met with his court appointed lawyer. The man wasn't as Glen imagined a lawyer should be. His jacket was creased, his fingers stained yellow by nicotine, and his belly strained at his shirt buttons.

"Are you guilty?"

Glen had already thought this through a hundred times. What good could come of any more truth. Secrets protected people. Alessandra wanted to die. She wouldn't have wanted him to rot in a prison cell, for their daughter to be to an orphan once more.

"No, I'm not."

"I must advise you that pleading not guilty is a risky strategy. If they can build a strong enough case and convince a jury, you could die in this place before you are ever released. I strongly recommend that you instruct me to negotiate with the prosecutor. I'm sure they would accept a guilty plea to manslaughter due to provocation, now that your wife's mother has spoken to them. You could be out in a few years."

"My wife's mother? What did she have to say?"

"That your daughter isn't yours. That she, your wife, was already pregnant when you met. That you didn't know this. She claims your wife must have finally told you, and that could be why you pushed her into the canal."

Glen sat back in his chair and put his hands on his head. It confirmed the answer to one question. Isabella wasn't his. Though why his mother-in-law had accused him of disgracing her daughter when they first met made no sense. Maybe she'd done so to help remove any lingering doubt which he might have had at the time that he wasn't the father, or perhaps Alessandra hid Isabella's true parentage from her mother also until, at some point, she had confided in the woman.

"But surely she wouldn't want her own granddaughter's paternity questioned in open court. For her to know that her father was a war criminal. A man who sent children to death camps."

"So it's true?"

"It's true I'm not her father. It's not true that I didn't know until recently," lied Glen.

"Well, you have a point. She might not be willing to appear for the reasons you've given. However, may

I put feelers out to the prosecutor? Nothing need be admitted unless a deal is done and approved by you."

"Okay."

The Vice Consul came to visit again. Glen gave him a letter he had written to Isabella and one for Dora. Only Dora replied.

Dear Glen

Thank you for your letter. Isabella left without telling anyone when I wasn't there. Neighbours say they saw her leaving with an older woman in a taxi. The police have since confirmed that she is with her grandmother in Italy.

The tragedy of Alessandra's death has made me do a lot of thinking. Whatever the truth may be, I have decided that you and I are just not meant to be together.

I'm moving away again. This time it will be for good, for everyone's sake.

Take care of yourself,

Dora

Not long afterwards came news from the bank that his services were being terminated. Glen wondered if the quagmire his life had become could get any deeper. It was as though the mud of the lagoon had hold of his feet and an incoming tide would soon overwhelm him.

What did it matter if they tried him for murder and convicted him? Isabella had ignored his letters from prison. Dora was gone. No one cared what happened to him, and nor did he any longer.

Winter incarcerated in Giudecca was long and bitter. The damp of the season seeped into his soul. In Dante's Inferno, Giudecca appears as the centre of Hell. Here Judas, along with Brutus and Cassius, are forever devoured by Satan. Things weren't quite that bad but it was an extremely grim few months. Venetians mock the island, calling its inhabitants 'seals' for their ability to tolerate the icy winds. The winds had no trouble finding their way into his tiny cell. His every joint ached and he was always cold.

The warmth of spring when it came didn't lift Glen's mood. Through his window, he could see the city across the water, smudged by winter's unwashed storms on the glass, like one of Turner's paintings of Venice.

La Serenissima tormented him. Not less than a mile away, people were marvelling at Tintorettos and Titians, sipping Bellinis, and enjoying themselves. Once again he found himself confined by the city. This time not as a war hero but as a murderer.

Then, mercurial like always, she released him. On this occasion it wasn't with fanfare down the Grand Canal, only a quick visit from his lawyer.

The prosecutor had dropped the case. The plea bargain of manslaughter due to provocation, which he'd offered and Glen's lawyer had advised him to accept, had been rejected by Glen.

His lawyer suspected Signora Faccini must have changed her story, unwilling to reveal who her granddaughter's real father was in open court, or that the prosecution had concluded she wouldn't be a convincing witness. He congratulated Glen on his perspicacity.

Glen's possessions were returned to him and he was taken by police boat to Marco Polo airport and a flight home. His protestations that he needed to go to Verona were ignored.

Home didn't feel like home any more. Isabella had filled the house with life and meaning. Now it was only a place to sleep. Sometimes when he awoke in the morning, he expected to hear her running down the stairs, calling for him or her mother. But there was nothing but overwhelming silence as if she had never lived here. It made him sad and empty, a man without purpose.

Neighbours expressed their condolences as he passed them in the street. But they had their doubts, he was certain of it. No smoke without fire, he heard two of them comment when they thought him out of earshot. When he walked into the Scott Arms pub, whispers were exchanged at the bar by locals who thought he wouldn't realise he was the subject of their discussion.

Glen applied for jobs in London. It would be easier to become a recluse there. No one would ask any questions or make any judgments. People would leave him alone, and that was what he wanted.

He found a position as an office administrator in

Holborn, and rented a small flat in Fulham. Work became his life and the tube journey from home to work and back delineated the extent of his world.

Glen stopped writing to Isabella after five letters remained unanswered, although he continued sending a card and a gift at Christmas and also in February on the date which she believed, and he used to believe, was her birthday.

It didn't matter to him that she wasn't his biological daughter. His initial rage and feeling of betrayal had long since dissipated. Isabella was his, not Schulte's. Glen had brought her up. He had loved her and cared for her. Schulte didn't even know she existed, and even if he had he wouldn't have been a proper father. He would have left Isabella in the orphanage without a second thought. Glen still loved her just as much. None of what had happened was her fault.

He went to see a lawyer about getting her back. It would be very expensive, the lawyer told him, and take a long time. Because of her age, the Italian courts would ask Isabella what she wanted. Given that she had ignored all his approaches, it seemed unlikely she would agree to live with him. Glen took the lawyer's advice and dropped the idea.

She would be sixteen now, almost a grown woman. It would soon be two years since he'd seen her. He resolved that he would go to see her and reason with her. A life of never seeing her was no life.

On the train from Milan, Glen thought about what he would say. Outside the entrance to her grandmother's apartment block in Verona, he stood, rehearsing his words. Breathing in deeply, he unclenched his fists and tried to calm his nerves. His finger hovered uncertainly above the buzzer as though he would set off a piercing alarm if he touched it. But waiting only made it worse. He pressed firmly.

CHAPTER 22

"Who is it?"
It wasn't the voice he'd hoped to hear but the strident tone of Signora Faccini.
"It's Glen. I want to talk to Isabella."
He pushed. The door didn't open. He pressed the buzzer again, several times. The door opened and Signora Faccini came out onto the street, letting the door close behind her. Her expression was one of revulsion, her eyes aflame with loathing.
"What do you think you're doing by coming here? She knows what you did, even if you got away with it. She doesn't want to see you again, ever. Stay away. Haven't you caused enough damage already?"
She didn't wait for a response and went back into the building, slamming the door as she went.
Glen looked up at the first floor. He thought he saw a face move quickly away from the window, though he couldn't be certain.
He walked down the street a little way and waited an hour, perhaps more. It began to rain heavily so he returned to his hotel.

Glen spent two more days in Verona, visiting every shop and cafe in the vicinity, just in case. Like a Cold War spy waiting for a handover of microfilm, he spent more hours at the end of her street. She never came or went. He could stay no longer, his flight was leaving Milan that evening.

Back in London, Glen tried to forget. Sometimes he succeeded for a day, sometimes two. He kept sending at Christmas and birthdays, hoping for a result like someone who still buys a lottery ticket every week, even though they know in their heart that they have a greater chance of being struck by lightning.

Colleagues at work told him he needed to meet someone. They even set him up with a few dates. There was Patricia from Putney. Glen visited her house once. She had cats, five of them. They made him sneeze uncontrollably and he had to leave after only ten minutes. There was Dorothy from Notting Hill who loved ballroom dancing. She told Glen that he had two left feet and it couldn't possibly work after he stood on her toes twice in the same evening. And there was Edith from Paris who spent half the year at her flat in Kensington. Glen liked her. She had a wicked sense of humour and great style. But she was in demand and dumped him after a few dates for the defence attaché at the American embassy.

Glen decided to give up on any further dating and closed his mind to love. He went back to watching television every evening. It was his best friend. His life might be boring but Glen was in his comfort zone and saw no reason to stray beyond it.

He ate dinner from a plate on his lap. He never sat at the table. It seemed too formal and accentuated his loneliness. The years passed. Glen developed a bald circle on his head and struggled to keep his ear hairs and eyebrows under control.

Isabella would be twenty-five now. Was she married? Did she have children of her own? Glen had resigned himself to the fact that he would never know.

He sometimes wondered what would happen when he got old and retired, without work to fill his days.

1971

It was an October evening when the telephone rang. It rarely did, and never this late. It was probably a wrong number. Glen tutted with annoyance. The call was interrupting 'Dad's Army', one of his favourite programmes. He balanced his dinner plate on the arm of his chair, and went across the room to pick up the phone.

"Hello."

The line crackled and the voice sounded distant. Glen couldn't understand what was being said. He was about to put the phone down when it dawned on him that the woman was speaking in Italian.

"Sorry, can you say that again. It's a bad line. I didn't get that."

He was pleased with himself that he could still

speak the language after so many years.

"Who's died?... Your sister?... Can you speak louder... Milena? Alessandra's aunt?... Yes, I remember you...Oh my god... Would you be able to send them to me? I'll send you the money for the postage...Oh, that's very kind...Do you know where Isabella is?...Oh... It was very good of you to get in touch. It means a lot... Thank you...You too...Goodbye."

Glen turned the television off and flopped back into his chair, knocking his dinner onto the floor in the process. He ignored it. This was incredible news.

His mother-in-law had died last week. While going through her things, her sister had found all the letters and cards which he had sent Isabella over the years unopened in a locked drawer in the woman's bedroom. So Isabella hadn't known how much he cared. She probably hadn't even refused to see him when he went to Verona. He slapped the arm of his chair in triumph, creating a small cloud of dust as he did so.

Maybe she would be willing to meet him if he could find her. Milena had explained Isabella had fallen out with her grandmother a few years ago and left, saying only that she was going to Venice. The family had heard nothing from her since.

Glen decided immediately he would go to Venice in an effort to find her. How he would track her down he didn't know but he must try.

His frugal lifestyle had allowed him to accumulate

significant savings so money wouldn't be an issue. He would ask for unpaid leave. If they refused, he would resign and find another job when he got back. Nothing mattered more than finding his darling Issie and getting a chance to talk to her at long last.

Years of the daily grind which had worn him down seemed to fall away. For once, Glen had a spring in his step and pushed his rounded shoulders back, a man energised and alive again.

The following week a parcel arrived from Verona. Tied together with a piece of string were twenty or so envelopes, his letters, birthday cards and Christmas cards. Signora Faccini's revenge for the death of her daughter. The envelopes were now showing their age and had begun to turn yellow.

While the Alitalia DC-9 made its final approach to Marco Polo airport, Glen could see the familiar roofs of Venice, a soft orange expanse anchored in the lagoon. Returning produced mixed emotions. He had experienced happiness here, but pain and captivity too.

Somewhere down there, in those narrow streets, his daughter could be walking, sitting at a cafe, or maybe serving a customer. So near yet so far.

The vaporetto from the airport zigzagged around the lagoon. It went first to the island of Burano, then to the Ospedale stop in the east of Venice by the hospital where Signor Ferraro used to work. Just as Glen thought he would soon reach his destination, the boat left Venice altogether and headed all the way out to the Lido before finally heading back to the city.

Glen was frustrated, it would have been much quicker if he had got off at Ospedale and walked the less than half a mile to the hotel. It was already dark when the boat finally arrived at San Zaccaria. Glen disembarked, weaving his way with his bag through the crowds still walking along Riva degli Schiavoni.

Inside the Danieli tranquility reigned, an oasis of calm from the hustle and bustle outside its door. He had reserved a room at the back of the hotel to reduce cost, but the woman at the front desk upgraded him to a room with a view of the water.

The bellboy, though he was no boy, opened the door with a flourish. Glen tipped him and sat on the bed. The room looked familiar. He realised he'd been here before. It was the very same one in which he and Alessandra stayed all those years ago after their trip to Lake Garda.

Glen wondered if the spirit of Alessandra was watching, smiling maybe and willing him on to success. He hoped so. He would need some special luck to find their daughter, assuming even that she was still here in Venice.

Glen went downstairs and sat in the lounge. Beneath a delicate but somewhat gaudy chandelier of Murano glass, he drank an amaretto and considered his plan. Each morning, he would get up early and stand at a different arrival point for the vaporetti bringing in workers. There was a good chance Isabella didn't actually live in Venice itself. Most workers commuted now. Venetian rents were beyond their reach.

One day he would try Santa Lucia, in case she came in by train from the mainland, and another Piazzale Roma to watch those arriving by bus. Then, when the rush hour ended, he would walk each calle, visit each campo and campiello, stopping in every shop and every bar to enquire if she worked there or if they recognised her photo. The one he possessed was over ten years old but it was the most recent he had.

It might be little better than trying to find a needle in a haystack but he had to start somewhere. The idea of going to the police was one he'd ruled out. If they searched their records, they were more likely to unearth information about him, and who knew if they could have changed their mind. Unlikely perhaps, but not a risk he was willing to take, for now at least.

The following morning, Glen was up and waiting at the San Zaccaria stop near the Danieli by six thirty to watch the boats come in and observe passengers disembarking. Three hours later, with his back aching from standing for so long, he retreated to the Danieli for a coffee and some breakfast.

Then he began his trek through the streets. He methodically marked them off on his map, one by one. There are about three thousand in total, connected by some three hundred and forty bridges over the canals. Glen had a lot of ground to cover.

As he went, he stared at young female passers by. Some shook their heads with indignation. He attempted to be more subtle. To them, he probably came across as a dirty old man. They couldn't know that he was only a father desperately trying to find his daughter.

"No, Signor" became the human interaction of his days. Initial enthusiasm became weary resignation. Several days later and he hadn't got a hint of recognition, not even an 'I'm not sure but there is a girl who looks a little like that.'

Then, out of the blue late one morning while he reconnoitred yet another street, Glen saw her. She crossed only a few metres in front of him where another alley intersected the one where he was standing. He hurried after her.

Her hair was much shorter, but that profile, that face, it had to be her. She walked with elegance and her clothes looked expensive. Glen pushed past a couple of ambling tourists to get to her.

"Issie! Issie! Stop. It's dad."

Everything became bright, too bright. Dizzy, Glen began to lose his balance. The world was spinning. He leaned his back against the wall for support.

CHAPTER 23

"Issie?"
"Are you all right?"
His vision came back into focus. The young woman was beside him.
"Yes. Thank you. I'm sorry, I thought you were my daughter."
"Maybe you should sit down and have some water. There's a cafe right here. Come, take my arm."
The young woman led him into a cafe and sat him down while she went to the counter to get him a San Pellegrino.
"How much do I owe you?"
"Forget it. You need to rest a little."
She sat opposite him. He felt foolish but she did bear a resemblance, quite a strong one.
"Are you searching for your daughter?"
"Yes, I am. We haven't seen each other for some years, but I believe she's in Venice so I've come to find her. Let me show you her photograph, just in case."
He pulled it out of his jacket pocket.
She smiled. "Your daughter is beautiful but I'm

afraid I haven't seen her."
"She looks like you in many ways."
"Yes, I suppose she does a bit. I'll ask around. See if I have a doppelgänger. They say we all do. Where can I contact you?"
"I'm staying at the Danieli. Glen Butler's my name."
"I thought I could detect a slight English accent but I must congratulate you, your Italian is excellent. I'm Gabriele. I'm studying at the German centre for Venetian studies. I'm sure you could detect my terrible German accent."
"No, your Italian is perfect. I really mustn't take up any more of your time. Thank you so much for your kindness."
"It's been a pleasure. You should take it easy for a while. I do hope you find her soon."
Glen followed Gabriele's advice and rested that day. Two days later when he returned exhausted to the hotel from another long day of fruitless search, the receptionist came running after him waving a note as Glen climbed the stairs feeling every one of his fifty years.

Dear Mr Butler

A fellow student tells me that a young woman working in Bacaro Siciliano in San Polo looks somewhat like me.
I'm keeping my fingers crossed for you,

Gabriele

Vitality returned to Glen's body, like rain falling on

parched earth. He took the remaining steps two by two. Back in his room, Glen rested a short while then headed back out. Covering the city sestiere by sestiere, San Polo was a district he hadn't even started on. But he didn't curse or complain, he was just grateful she had been found, grateful that she was still in Venice.

He crossed the Rialto bridge and worked his way through the myriad of lanes to where the hotel concierge said he would find the bar. Sweating profusely from his walk and his apprehension that she might tell him to leave and never bother her again, he pushed on the heavy wooden door.

The bacaro was narrow and lined with dark wood. There was standing room only as locals imbibed small glass beakers of wine and stabbed at the cicchetti laid out on the bar counter with toothpicks. A haze of smoke from their cigarettes languidly drifted around the bar. Ancient looking copper pots of various sizes hung from the ceiling. The place oozed Venice, real Venice, with not a tourist in sight.

A tall man in a black shirt was busy serving behind the bar but Glen couldn't see Isabella. The man looked surprised when he saw Glen, someone who clearly wasn't a Venetian.

"Yes?" he asked with irritation, probably assuming this man could only have come in to ask for directions.

"I believe a young woman by the name of Isabella works here."

"No."

Glen fumbled in his pocket and got out the now crumpled photo he had shown hundreds of times before.

"Was this taken many years ago?" asked the barman, frowning while he examined it as though trying to imagine what she must look like now.

"Yes."

"It could be Bianca. She has the day off. Why do you ask? Who are you?"

Glen hesitated. A change of name. She didn't want to be found.

"No, it can't be her. I'm sorry to have troubled you. Thanks anyway."

By eleven the following morning, Glen had set himself up in a cafe diagonally opposite the bar.

Around noon she arrived. Her long brown hair was gone. It was short, ending just below her ears and dyed a bright auburn. It looked as though she'd probably cut it herself. She wore an oversized green coat which was faded, like something from an army surplus store and laced brown boots, a far cry from the Italian fashionista who he thought she might have become.

Conflicting emotions of happiness and sadness battled inside him. The last time he'd seen her she was in her early teens, now she was a fully grown woman. He had missed all those years, never seeing her once. He wanted to rush out and hug her, tell her how he loved her. But he restrained himself. She was about to start work. He wanted time to talk when she wasn't in a hurry.

All day long he waited. Sometimes walking up and down outside, but mostly inside the cafe across the street until they closed at six. After that he waited on the street, sitting with his back against the wall like a homeless person when his legs had grown too tired to remain standing any longer. A few passers by even threw him some coins.

His watch told him that he'd been there twelve hours. He hoped her shift would soon end.

Shortly after midnight she came out of the bar, turning away from where he was towards the fish market. In the shadows of the night, thin cats picked on fragments of fish left behind and the pavement gave off a heavy odour.

She walked briskly. He followed, struggling to keep up.

"Issie. Wait."

She turned.

"Issie, it's me. Dad."

He had hoped to see a flicker of warmth, a hint that she was pleased to see him.

CHAPTER 24

"What are you doing here? Go away and leave me alone."

She kept going, passing under deserted arches by the Grand Canal. Glen chased after her until he overtook her. Breathless, he stood in front of her forcing her to halt.

"I wanted you to have these. It's all the letters and cards I sent you. Your grandmother hid them from you. Her sister found them when she died."

Isabella betrayed no emotion as she took them from him. She went around him and carried on walking.

"I'm staying at the Danieli. I would love to have the chance to talk to you. To explain…"

She'd already turned a corner, leaving him staring at an empty space.

Each time Glen passed the front desk at the hotel, he enquired if there were any messages for him. He was convinced that once she read those cards and letters, she would have a change of heart.

Two days after their encounter, the concierge handed him an envelope. Glen tore it open. At last, a message from Isabella. But it wasn't from her. It was from Gabriele.

Dear Mr. Butler

I hope that you found your daughter.
My father is over from Germany. I think he would appreciate the company of someone nearer his own age.
We are having dinner this evening at 8 at Ristorante Marcella near Centro Tedesco di Studi Veneziani. It would be so wonderful if you could join us.
If you found your daughter, please do bring her along. It would be lovely to meet her.

Best wishes

Gabriele

Glen screwed the message up and put it in his pocket. Five more times that day he went to the front desk, but there was no word from Isabella.

He went out for a walk. It was a pleasant October evening. Glen wasn't paying much attention to where he was going. Feeling hungry he looked for a place to eat. He noticed that he wasn't that far from the Marcella. It was shortly after eight o'clock. Glen decided a night of not eating alone for once might help ease the gnawing restlessness inside of him which greeted him first thing each morning and stayed with him all day long.

"I'm so glad you came," said Gabriele when he approached their table. "Did you-"

"Yes. Thank you so much for helping. She wasn't able to come." A lie was easier than an explanation. "This is my father."

A portly man a few years older looking than Glen, wiped his hands on his napkin and half stood to offer his hand. His fingers were like sausages, his grip tight. His face was round and flushed, but jovial. Glen imagined him to be some jolly Bavarian farmer type. Someone who was never happier than when leading his cattle up into Alpine meadows.

"Schulte. Delighted to meet you."

The name went through Glen like a fork of lightning. He grabbed the back of the chair for support.

"Are you feeling all right?" asked Gabriele.

"Yes. Another one of those dizzy spells, it'll soon pass. I probably need to eat something."

"That's what we're here for," chuckled Schulte in his heavily accented Italian. "Have some wine."

Glen didn't remember much of the dinner or conversation. While he answered Schulte's questions he couldn't stop thinking about how the man opposite him was Isabella's true father, and the woman next to him her half sister. Schulte, evil personified, here in the flesh, sitting right in front of him. A war criminal. Alive and well. Unrepentant. Unpunished.

Glen drank to suppress the rage inside. It didn't work so he drank some more. He was fast becoming inebriated.

"I'm afraid I must go now, I'm meeting some friends. We're working weekends at the German pavilion at the Biennale this month and need to agree on who does which dates. I'll leave you two to share stories of Venice. See you later, Vati. Thank you for coming, Mr Butler."

"I have some excellent schnapps back at the apartment. How about we go there? You can tell me more about how you hid from us in Venice. Thank God we are all friends now."

Friends? This vile person would never be a friend. Glen wanted to reach across the table and pick him up by the collar and choke him but it was too public here. Glen accepted his invitation. The apartment was a short walk away.

"I rent this for my daughter," said Shulte opening the door. "It's also handy for when I come to visit. I'd like to come more often but my printing business demands nearly all my time. Make yourself comfortable while I pour us some drinks." The flat had a strong Germanic air. On the walls were paintings of whitewashed churches with their distinctive onion domes, Bavarian villages with half-timbered buildings, and snowy mountain peaks. Not a thing was out of place.

Schulte busied himself pouring generous glasses of schnapps. Glen watched him from behind, like a leopard eyeing a warthog and getting ready to pounce.

"There we go," said Schulte as he turned to pass Glen his glass.

Glen pushed him forcefully in the chest. Schulte tottered backwards, spilling the drinks.

"What are you doing?"

"I know who you are, Schulte. You're a murderer, that's what you are. You sent Jews to their deaths. You had people executed. You're nothing but scum. I expect you thought you'd got away with it, huh? That you could wash your hands of your past. Well, not any longer. I'm going report you to Simon Wiesenthal, the Nazi hunter. Your respectable little life in Germany is over. You'll finally have to pay for your crimes."

"I don't know what you're talking about. Have you lost your mind?"

"Absolutely not. You seduced my wife, Alessandra Faccini, and then cast her aside like a piece of rubbish. Remember? Had her boss, Signor Lamberti executed for sheltering a harmless little boy and a girl, and sent them off to die in the gas chambers.

"I have never heard of these people."

Schulte picked up a silver candle stick from the sideboard next to him. "You're deranged. I offer you friendship but you make terrible allegations and assault me. Get out."

Glen didn't move. Schulte swung the candle stick clumsily at him. Glen crouched down to avoid it. Coming back up, he swung a punch, hitting Schulte on the chin.

Schulte staggered backwards in slow motion before falling and landing on his back while his legs gave way under him. He lay there like a giant upturned beetle, unable to right himself and scurry off to safety.

Glen jumped on him and sat astride him. He raised Schulte's head by pulling on his shirt with one hand so that he could pummel him.

All the anger and frustration which Glen felt at what had happened in his life, he channelled into the punches he threw. He only stopped when Schulte passed out, bloody and bruised. Glen got up to leave. The room was spinning. He fell on the floor next to Schulte in a drunken stupor.

When he came to, Gabriele had returned. She was kneeling next to her father.

"Bist du okay?"

"Ja," he replied weakly

She turned to look at Glen who was getting up from the floor. "Why did you do this to him?" Her expression was one of anger and contempt.

"Gabriele, there's something that you need to know about your father, Gunther Schulte. He was in the Gestapo. He rounded up people and sent them to the gas chambers."

CHAPTER 25

"What! You didn't even bother to ask his name? My father's name is Karl. Gunther was my uncle. He's dead. He died last year. My father was an ordinary soldier. He hated the Nazis." Glen was lost for words. "Go! Just get out of here. I never want to see you again."

Glen headed back towards the hotel. He resolved to return to London, ready to accept defeat. Isabella wanted nothing to do with him. He would have to adjust to that and move on. He had placed his entire life on hold for years in the hope he would find her and they could put things back together again. Now he'd just attacked and nearly killed an innocent man. Enough was enough.

This city, which had once seduced him so, had become a curse, always dragging him back to the past. A past which he couldn't change. How different his life would be if he had never set foot here.

Glen entered the Danieli. He didn't even have to ask the front desk any longer.

"No messages Signor," the concierge volunteered.

"I'm leaving tomorrow. Can you let reception know for me."

The following morning, Glen took a leisurely breakfast on the roof terrace. His flight wasn't until late in the afternoon.

Venice looked at her best from up here, her modern day blemishes hidden from view. The tourist hordes were invisible, the tacky souvenir shops out of sight, the garish picture menus still put away from the night before. From here, she exuded a serenity long since abandoned at street level in pursuit of the tourist Dollar, Deutsch Mark, and Yen.

"Signor, a message. The man from front desk stood by his table offering him an envelope.

"Thank you," said Glen reaching inside his pocket for a tip.

He dropped the coins, his nerves having got the better of him. Once he had retrieved them and the concierge had left, he examined the envelope.

Glen Butler, Hotel Danieli.

He recognised her handwriting, spider like and leaning forwards as if dominoes lined up vertically and all toppling one after another from the tap of a finger. It was one thing which she'd forgotten to change in seeking to eradicate all traces of her former identity.

As though receiving exam results, wanting the news to be good but fearing the worst, he held the envelope for a while, turning it in his hands in the hope it might make the message inside a positive one. Finally overcoming his apprehension, he opened it.

The paper came out with the writing on the other side. However, it was thin and he could see there was just one line of script. His heart sank. Rejection.

But when he turned it over, he grinned.

Meet me at the cafe opposite the bacaro at 11 Thursday morning.

There was no 'Dear Papa', no signature, no love, no kisses, but it was something. A chance to talk. What more could he expect at this stage? Yesterday's decision to submit to defeat was replaced by the allure of hope.

Glen was at the cafe twenty minutes early. Isabella was fifteen minutes late. She wore the same faded green coat she'd been wearing the day he'd found her. Glen greeted her with a smile and asked what she would like to drink. She said a coffee, but there was no smile in return.

"Did you read the letters?"

"Yes, but you didn't tell me what I wanted to know."

"What was that?"

"Did you kill Mama?"

Glen opened his mouth but hesitated.

"Well, did you? It's a simple enough question."

"She wanted me to. When we reached the hotel, she told me she needed my help to kill herself. She said she didn't want to go on living. Get to the stage where she would be utterly helpless, and end up choking on her saliva."

Isabella turned her head sideways to try and hide her emotion. Glen touched her hand which was resting on the table. She quickly withdrew it.

"I did what she wanted me to."

Glen couldn't give her the whole truth. Tell her that he wasn't her real father. Tell her how he had lost his temper and pushed her mother's wheelchair towards the canal making no attempt to stop it, only because she'd told him Isabella wasn't related to him by blood. Tell her how he had told Alessandra that she had ruined his life, robbed him of happiness with Dora.

Isabella fixed him with a stare. "Or was it that you wanted her out of the way?"

"I don't know what you mean."

"I saw you kissing Dora the day you left for Venice. How could you have done that? Mama needed you and you were carrying on with another woman behind her back."

"It wasn't like that."

"Just what was it like then?"

"Your mother knew about it. She approved of it. You see, Dora was the woman who I was engaged to marry when your mother got in touch to tell me you had been born and were being kept by the nuns in an orphanage. Back then, unmarried women couldn't keep their babies. I came to Verona and married your mother so that we could get you out of the orphanage. I tried to love her. I didn't see Dora for years. Then that summer when we went to Garda and you and your mother stayed on while I came home, that's when I met her again. When you came back I was going to tell your mother, tell her I was leaving but that's when she became ill and I couldn't. Your mother guessed. She told me she wanted me to be happy. She even suggested Dora help look after her so she could get to know you, for the time when she would no longer be around."

Glen couldn't see Isabella's face. She'd placed her hand on her forehead to shield her eyes, but he heard a soft plop as a tear fell into her coffee.

"I'm so sorry, Isabella. So sorry that you've been hurt and alone. Your mother and I both loved you so much, and I always will. I came to Verona when you were about sixteen. Your grandmother said you didn't want to see me. When her sister rang me after she died to tell me she'd hidden everything I ever sent you, and told me the last they knew was that you were in Venice, I came here to look for you. I want to be here for you, Issie. I want to try and make up for what happened."

She wiped her hand across her face, sniffed hard and stood up. "I have to go now."

"Can I see you again?"

"I don't know."

"When's your next day off?"

"Sunday."

"I'll be outside the Accademia at noon. Please come

if you can."

Her face wrinkled with a mixture of pain and confusion, Isabella didn't answer. She left half running, half walking.

CHAPTER 26

Before Sunday, there was something Glen wanted to do. He took a boat from Fondamente Nuove on the east side of Venice across the short stretch of water to San Michele. For over a hundred years it had been Venice's city of the dead, ever since the former practice of burying the departed under the city's paving stones was banned for reasons of public health.

The tightly packed boat approached the apricot-orange walls behind which dark cypresses swayed in the breeze. Glen clutched three bunches of flowers he had bought. He'd chosen chrysanthemums, the flowers for the dead in Italy. Disembarking, he found a warden and, after explaining when they had died, asked him where they might be buried.

"It's most unlikely you will find the son. This place is overflowing with the dead. Normally after that long, the body will have been exhumed and the bones taken to an ossuary on the mainland or cremated if that is what his parents requested. More recent graves for Catholics are over that way," he pointed.

The place was a maze of headstones and flowers. In the Italian tradition, by each grave was a photograph of the deceased. It gave a heightened sense of poignancy to the location. These graves weren't merely inscriptions to faceless people as in England.

Glen walked along row after row until he found it. One grave, two pictures. They had died within days of each other three years earlier. He carefully laid down two bunches of flowers in memory of Doctor Ferraro and his wife.

"Farewell, my dear friends. I hope you're now reunited with your sons. I'll remember you and what you did for me always."

While his boat returned him to the city, Glen threw the last bunch of chrysanthemums on the water in memory of Luca. They floated away, taken by the outgoing tide. The sadness which had accompanied Glen that day intensified while he thought how Luca dreamt of taking a transatlantic liner out of this very lagoon to a new life in America. So many dreams of the youth of his generation unfulfilled, washed out to sea and lost.

On Sunday morning, Glen arrived outside the Accademia early. He soon realised his suggestion of a venue could have been better. The throng of visitors outside one of the world's great art collections would make it hard to see her if she came. He moved his head from side to side constantly, like a flamingo looking for its young but with none of its grace.

There was a tap on his shoulder.

"Did you want to see the paintings?" he asked

"No, they depict the rich and powerful. Those who exploited the masses, exactly as is still happening today."

"Oh," was all Glen could manage to say. He wasn't interested in politics and never expected his daughter would be.

"I only have half an hour. Let's get a coffee," she said.

At a cafe in a side street in Dorsoduro behind the Accademia, they sat outside.

"Where do you live?"

"In Guidecca, just back from Palanca. Above a bar."

How ironic, thought Glen, that his daughter should be living not far from the prison where he had once been held.

"Do you have any plans?"

"Plans?"

"Work wise."

"What? You mean you think I ought to work in a bank like you."

"No, I didn't mean that."

"Good, because I don't believe in the capitalist system which makes the rich richer and keeps the poor enslaved. Did you know the Nazis who you fought against merely reinvented themselves after the war? They persuaded the United States they were a lesser evil than the Soviets. They made the world fear communism more than fascism, to enable them to infiltrate and control the levers of power. They've even kept their shrine right here in this city."

"I've never been into politics myself. I did read though that Italy has a big communist party."

"They're no better than the rest of them, only more pigs with their snouts in the trough."

Glen decided to try and steer things in another direction. His daughter's conversation was like receiving a lecture from Fidel Castro or Mao Zedong. He was here to spend precious time with her, not change the world.

"I like your hair, the way you have it. Shorter."

"I was tired of having it meet bourgeois expectations. It's utilitarian, unimportant."

Glen wondered who could have made her like this, so automated, so joyless in her outlook on life.

"I take it you're not married."

"I wouldn't want to be. It's an outmoded institution used to oppress women."

"Issie-"

"My name's Bianca now."

"I only want to chat and get to know you again. My questions aren't meant to offend you."

"There's a man I live with if that's what you want to know."

"What does he do?"

"Look, I don't think this is going to work. I'm not the girl you once knew. I need to go."

"Please don't."

But she had already pushed her chair back. "I can't

do this."

Glen got up too but he could see it was useless. He watched her leave. She didn't look back, not even once.

Glen walked across the wooden bridge by the Accademia in the direction of the hotel. An emptiness which felt like the pressure of deep water crushed him. By the time he reached the church of San Moise, it was as though he was breathing through a straw. The church's over elaborate facade, which had the appearance of a wedding cake with way too much decoration, seemed to come alive and jump out at him as if he were hallucinating.

A sharp pain began in his chest. He put his hand on it in a vain attempt to make it go away and fell to his knees.

CHAPTER 27

Glen didn't remember much after that apart from a vague recollection of being lifted onto a stretcher and hurried to an ambulance boat waiting by the nearest canal.

Now he was lying in a hospital bed. A monitor beeped, like a monosyllabic bird tweet but without the happiness, and a tube was attached to his arm. A nurse came over to his bed. "How are you feeling?"

"A little out of sorts. What happened?"

"The doctor will be here soon to explain. You should rest."

Glen realised that he must be getting old. The doctor looked the same age as Isabella.

"You had a heart attack. We need to keep you in for a while, for observation. It's important that you avoid stress and take only gentle exercise. The strain on your heart could be too great. You might not survive next time. Is there family we can contact for you?"

"No, no one. I live alone. I'm on holiday from England. I'm staying at the Danieli."

"Do you want us to phone the hotel and have anything sent over?"

"No. That won't be necessary, thank you."

"Right. The nurse will need to take a few details from you. I'll see you later."

After three days, Glen was discharged. He'd been told not to fly for another few days. Having had his mortality thrust centre stage, Glen decided that he must make one last effort to see Isabella. Life was too short, too fragile not to try. He didn't want to go home to die, be it soon or in many years time, thinking if only, if only he had spoken to his daughter once more and found a way to establish some kind of relationship between them.

The evening of the day he was released from hospital he took a vaporetto across the water to Giudecca. Here was another Venice, one which few tourists saw. No Florian café or Harry's Bar. No grand palazzi. At the time it was like Venice's very own London's East End. The buildings still needed repair and renovation. It looked little different to his previous, involuntary visit when he'd come as a prisoner. Giudecca was bohemian maybe but not in a charming way.

There was a bar near Palanca. He went inside. Its wooden tables were old and etched with names and graffiti. A couple of posters hung from the walls. Communist party election posters from some years back, faded with age. One showed a young boy and girl, their faces were eerily adult looking. Behind them were the Soviet flag of hammer, sickle and a star, and the Italian tricolour. The other poster was of Lenin, his face red and appearing to glow like a warm fire against a black background.

Glen sat with a glass of red wine by the window. It wasn't long until she passed right in front of him, arm in arm with a man. Glen shrank back as they turned to come in. He wanted to speak to her alone. But they didn't come in, they entered a door right next to the bar's entrance.

He waited a few minutes and then downed what remained of his wine in one gulp. Outside, he knocked using the door knocker, a brass lion's head.

The door opened but it wasn't his daughter. A man, much larger than Glen, with stubble and unruly black hair which covered his ears in the fashion of the times, stood there glaring at him.

"Who are you? What do you want?"

"I'm Isa-, Bianca's father. Can I talk to her please?"

"No, she doesn't want to see you." He slammed the door.

Glen knocked again. The man's expression was no more friendly than a bear warning against approaching its cub.

"Fuck off old man and leave her alone. Knock again and you'll regret it."

Glen heeded the advice. His goal was unachievable. He slipped an envelope under the door, recalling the words which he had written below his address and telephone number in London.

My dearest Isabella,

I'm very grateful to have seen you again and to have been able to explain things at long last.
I'm so sorry I wasn't there when you needed me most.
If ever you need anything, please, please get in touch.
I wish you all the happiness in the world. I will love you forever.

Your Papa

He walked away, regretting each step of separation.

Hasty footsteps from behind made him turn. It was her. But she hadn't come to throw her arms around him and tell him that she loved him too.

"You need to let me go. Not come back, ever. Go home to England and find a life. You can't live for Isabella. She doesn't exist any longer."

"I'm leaving. My flight's on Sunday."

"Good."

She moved to go but something made her hesitate.

"What is it?"

"Stay away from the Biennale on Saturday."

"Why?"

"It's not safe. Just stay away, and don't tell anyone I told you."

She hurried back the way she'd come. Glen didn't wait this time to see if she would look behind her for one last glance. He carried on walking towards the vaporetto stop.

Stay away from the Biennale. It's not safe. Those

words echoed in his head like the lyrics of a song that wouldn't leave him be. What had she got herself involved in? A demonstration, a protest perhaps. But why would she run after him to tell him to stay away from that, tell him that it wasn't safe. It didn't make sense.

Before retiring to bed, Glen went into the hotel lounge and ordered a limoncello. He picked up a copy of the *Corriere della Sera* lying on the coffee table, hoping that reading a newspaper might distract him for a while. He was tired but too wound up to sleep. The picture on the front page showed a body on a stretcher covered with a sheet, and a car which had crashed into a wall covered in bullet holes. Above it the headline read:

'Red Brigade claims responsibility for politician's murder in roadside shooting.'

Glen had never heard of the 'Brigate Rosso'. The newspaper described them as a left wing paramilitary organisation seeking to create a revolutionary state through armed struggle.

His heart rate quickened and his mouth went dry. Could it possibly be that Isabella and that unpleasant boyfriend of hers were members of the Red Brigade or something equally sinister? Her political views seemed extreme. Could they be planning an attack at the Biennale, Venice's contemporary art exhibition?

CHAPTER 28

She had told him to stay away. Leave her alone. He couldn't. That would be abandoning his responsibility as a father, as someone who cared about her.

Tomorrow he would go to the bar where she worked and confront her. Stop her doing anything stupid. She must have been brainwashed by her boyfriend or his accomplices. How else could she have become who she now was?

Glen waited outside on the street near Bacaro Siciliano. By noon Isabella still hadn't arrived. He went into the bar.

"Is Bianca working today?"

"She left," said the barman. "She gave her notice in last week."

"Do you know where she's working now?"

"No, she didn't say."

Glen walked back to the Rialto and caught a vaporetto to Palanca in Giudecca. There was no answer to his frantic knocking. He went into the bar next door to ask.

"They left this morning. They said they were

spending time with friends before leaving Venice, moving to Rome, apparently."
"Do you know where their friends live?"
"No."
Glen made his way back to the vaporetto stop. He didn't know what to do next. He could go to the Biennale himself tomorrow and try to stop her if he saw her. But the crowds would probably be big. It would be so easy to miss her.

He could go to the police, but then she would very likely end up in prison or worse. Yet could he risk letting innocent people die?

Glen got off the boat at Giardini and bought himself an entrance ticket. His fears were confirmed. The mass of visitors made it hard to see everyone arriving.

He didn't enter any of the over thirty national pavilions to look at the artwork. It was of no interest to him. What he needed was a clue of some kind. Why the Biennale? Because it attracted lots of people, or because she would view it as bourgeois maybe? But what would be their target?

The grounds were large. Glen trudged around despondently in the warm sunshine. Could his once sweet, innocent daughter actually have become someone who would engage in violence and hurt others? Her life should have been so different, so much better than this.

At the far end of the exhibition ground, Glen reached the German pavilion. He remembered reading about it. It was a controversial building.

There had been several calls to tear it down.
Built in the early 1900s, it had received a fascist make over in 1938 to correspond with Nazi architectural requirements. Its Ionic columns evoking ancient Greece were replaced by utilitarian columns conveying uncompromising Teutonic values. A more imposing roof had also been added.
It was here that Hitler and Mussolini had given their fascist salutes. Busts of the two leaders had been displayed alongside sculptures of perfect Aryan specimens. After the war, the swastikas and Nazi eagle were removed but the building remained, a defiant statement of fascism with no concession to the soothing architecture of Venice.
What was it Isabella had said? The Nazis never went away. They reinvented themselves, persuaded America that they were a lesser evil than the Russians. Their shrine remains in Venice. That must surely be it. They were going to launch an attack here at the German Pavilion.
And Gabriele. The girl who had found Isabella for him, hadn't she said she worked here at weekends? Glen walked briskly the mile or so to Gabriele's flat. Her brow creased in a scowl. "I thought I told you never to come back."
"I wanted to tell you that you and your friends need to stay away from the German Pavilion at the Biennale tomorrow."
"Why?"
"I can't say."

"You need help, you have mental health issues." She slammed the door in his face. Glen knew what he must do.

The police officer read from the notes he'd made in his notebook.

"You believe there is to be an attack at the Biennale tomorrow, most probably at the German pavilion. You fear that your daughter, who you are estranged from, has been radicalised by her boyfriend, who may be a member of the Red Brigade or some other far left terrorist group. That they and or others are planning to do this. She told you to stay away. That it wouldn't be safe. That the Nazi shrine remains in Venice."

"Yes, but I need you to keep your promise that you won't harm her. You won't shoot her."

"Wait here a moment."

He returned with a book of photographs. "Look at these and tell me if you recognise anyone."

Glen turned the pages. "This one, that's him. Her boyfriend."

"Do you know where they live?"

"I did but when I went there this morning they had left. Gone into hiding, I think."

"Well, tell me where they used to live. We'll want to see if they've left any clues behind."

Glen described the location.

"You have been extremely helpful, Mr Butler. If we need anything further, we will contact you at the Danieli. You are not to leave Venice without letting us know."

"I won't. And you will ensure that no harm comes to my daughter?"

"You have my word."

Glen struggled to eat his pasta at dinner. He had no appetite. He had betrayed Isabella. It gnawed at him, like maggots in his stomach, hundreds of them eating away at his very being. It was easy to claim justification for reporting her to the police, risking her life to save the lives of others. But that wasn't his true betrayal. He had betrayed her many years ago.

He could have resisted the urge to be with Dora. He could have put his daughter first. If he had controlled his temper when Alessandra told him the truth, he would have been there for Isabella. Her mother was dying, Isabella had needed his support more than ever.

But he'd been selfish, it was all about him, not his daughter. She had been left alone, without a parent to protect her and guide her. Who wouldn't have been deeply affected by her experience? Was it so surprising she'd become who she had, susceptible to manipulation and exploitation? And now she, the person he loved most, could end up paying the price for his mistakes.

CHAPTER 29

Sleep was impossible that night. Early morning, he drank two double espressos to revitalise himself. They did the trick but elevated his anxiety levels which were already dangerously high. Glen noticed that the rhythm of his heartbeat had become irregular. He told himself it must be the caffeine.

Glen left the hotel well before ten to be there for opening time. He walked east past the Arsenale, a place which had always fascinated him. The lion statues outside looked as though they should be Venetian but in fact had been looted from Delos and Piraeus in Greece. The world's first production line was created behind those crenellated brick walls where Venice once produced a ship every single day, far in advance of any competitor, making her master of the Eastern Mediterranean. Today, Glen didn't even give the Arsenale a glance. He had but one focus.

A couple of policemen stood by the entrance to the Biennale, to observe arrivals no doubt. Only a handful of people were in front of Glen in the queue forming to get in. Inside the grounds he couldn't spot any uniformed officers, but that didn't mean they weren't here in plain clothes so as not to scare off any would be attackers.

The numbers of visitors began to swell. He decided to position himself by the corner of the British Pavilion which was close to the neighbouring German one. Glen scrutinised those approaching like a hawk but they all looked harmless. There was laughter, chatter, and happy faces. Not a hint of trouble.

The hours passed. He began to let himself hope that whatever plan Isabella and that odious partner of hers may have hatched, they must have decided to abandon it.

Tourists stopped to watch the many street entertainers who sought to relieve them of their loose change. Some had dressed as though it was Carnevale in masks and elaborate costumes. The atmosphere was joyful and innocent.

A couple came along the path, posing for photographs. One was dressed as a Venetian plague doctor, his cloak black, his mask golden with a long, curved beak like that of some exotic bird. His costume was topped off by a wide-brimmed, black leather hat. Once that rather sinister outfit was thought to protect those administering to the sick from catching the plague. Now it was an icon of Venetian tourism.

His companion's costume was much more elaborate. Her face was covered by a white mask, with thick black edging around the eye holes and cherry red lips, as though she was a Venetian geisha. Her cloak, which also covered her head, and her dress were a deep vermillion, decorated with golden brocade. She curtsied obligingly to visitors taking her picture while the two masked figures slowly made their way amongst the crowd. The couple meandered towards the German Pavilion. Glen noticed they didn't seek money like the others, and didn't accept it even when it was offered.

His palms became clammy and his heart began to race. He instinctively reacted to his gut feeling.

"Isabella!" he cried and ran towards the woman.

The couple looked around, their masks concealing whatever their expression might be.

The woman stood still, unsure what to do. The man sprinted towards the German Pavilion.

Out of the corner of his eye, Glen saw two men emerge from behind the tree to the left of the entrance to the Pavilion. Both had guns.

One fired a shot at the plague doctor. He stumbled and then fell to the ground. The other raised his gun in the woman's direction.

"No!" shouted Glen throwing himself at her, knocking her down and landing on top of her.

There was a sharp pain in his chest. Another heart attack. This must be it. The one that would kill him. It didn't matter so long as she survived.

The woman wriggled out from under him and got up. Still on the ground, Glen rolled over to look at her. She pulled off her mask. He'd been right, it was his daughter.

Isabella knelt next to him, cradling him in her arms.

Glen noticed there was blood on her hands, but he was glad to see she hadn't been shot. The blood was coming from him.

He relaxed. Isabella would live. At last, he'd been there for her when she needed him.

Tears filled her eyes. "Papa."

That one word brought him peace. Almost. He needed to die without guilt. She deserved to know the truth.

Two policemen hovered above them, impatient to take his daughter away.

"One moment, please," said Glen. "Isabella, there's something you have a right to know, something which I've hidden from you. I'm not your real father. He was a German soldier. He's dead now.

"Your mother told me that I wasn't your father the last time I brought her to Venice, the day she died. At the hotel, she'd asked me to run a bath and leave her in it, and go down to the bar while she drowned herself. But I'd refused to help her kill herself.

"Maybe she finally told me the truth to make me angry, hoping I would kill her. Or it could have been that she too, knowing the illness would soon kill her, wanted to go with a clear conscience. I don't know.

"I reacted badly. We were by the side of a canal

when she told me. I pushed on the arms of her wheelchair in frustration. The brake wasn't on and it went backwards into the water. I didn't mean for that to happen, but I didn't try and stop it. I could have saved her. I'm so sorry."

"It's okay. You did what she wanted. She was ready to die. And I don't care about the German. I have only one father. You."

Glen heard her forgiveness and closed his eyes.

"Hold on, Papa. Please," she urged as the two men pulled her away and handcuffed her.

CHAPTER 30

1978

Her hand held his, tightly. Small fingers gripping his, a sensation more precious than all the spices and silks from the East which had once made Venice so wealthy.

It reminded him of when Isabella was little. How she had always held his hand then, had stayed faithfully by his side whenever they left the house. The man and young girl were waiting outside the women's prison on Giudecca. It was a cold February day. An icy wind blew down from the Dolomites and across the lagoon. Funnelled into their narrow street, it had a raw bite and stung their cheeks. Occasional snowflakes drifted lethargically down from a pewter sky. When they hit the ground, they dissolved on the wet paving. It was a place devoid of colour, a world of grey and decay.

The two of them paid no attention to the weather or their surroundings. Their thoughts were elsewhere. Those large doors opposite would open soon and she would emerge.

Although the little girl by his side would never know her real father, her grandfather adored her, and her mother loved her too.

Next week, the girl would be six. She wasn't worried about having a party and hadn't thought about what presents she might get. They would all be together, a family at last. And that would be the best present of all.

++++++++++++++++++++++++++++++++

ALSO BY DAVID CANFORD

The Shadows of Seville

A gripping and moving story of loss and love, of hatred and passion, and of horror and hope, set in Spain's most evocative city during the turmoil of the Spanish Civil War and the following decades. Lose yourself in vibrant 'Sevilla' where the shadows of the past are around every corner.

Puppets of Prague

Can the dream of freedom overcome fear and oppression? Friendships are tested to the limit in this saga spanning Prague's tumultuous 20th century. In the summer of 1914 young love beckons and the future seems bright for three close friends, but momentous events throw into stark relief the differences between them that had never mattered before.

Going Big or Small

British humour collides with European culture in this tale of 'it's never too late'. Retiree, Frank, gets more adventure than he bargained for when he sets off across 1980s Europe hoping to shake up his mundane life. Falling in love with a woman and Italy has unexpected consequences.

A Good Nazi? The Lies We Keep

Growing up in 1930s Germany two boys, one Catholic and one Jewish, become close friends. After Hitler seizes power, their lives are changed forever. When World War 2 comes, will they help each other, or will secrets from their teenage years make them enemies?

Kurt's War

Kurt is an English evacuee with a difference. His father is a Nazi. As Kurt grows into an adult and is forced to pretend that he is someone he isn't for his own protection, will he survive in the hostile world in which he must live? And with his enemies closing in, will even the woman he loves believe who he really is?

A Heart Left Behind

New Yorker, Orla, finds herself trapped in a web of secret love, blackmail and espionage in the build up to WW2. Moving to Berlin and hoping to escape her past, she is forced to undertake a task that will cost not only her own life but also that of her son if she fails.

The Throwback - The Girl who wasn't wanted

A baby's birth on a South Carolina plantation threatens to cause a scandal, but the funeral of mother and child seems to ensure that the truth will never be known. A family saga of hatred, revenge, forbidden love, overcoming hardship and helping others.

Bound Bayou

A young teacher from England achieves a dream when he gets the chance to work for a year in the United States, but 1950s Mississippi is not the America he has seen on the movie screens at home. When his independent spirit collides with the rules of life in the Deep South, he sets off a chain of events he can't control.

Sea Snakes and Cannibals

A travelogue of visits to islands around the world, including remote Fijian islands, Corsica, islands in the Sea of Cortez, Mexico, and the Greek islands.

When the Water Runs Out

Will water shortage result in the USA invading Canada? One person can stop a war if he isn't killed first but is he a hero or a traitor? When two very different worlds collide, the outcome is on a knife-edge.

2045 The Last Resort

In 2045 those who lost their jobs to robots are taken care of in resorts where life is an endless vacation. For those still in work, the American dream has never been better. But is all quite as perfect as it seems?

THANK YOU

I hope you enjoyed reading 'Betrayal in Venice'. I would appreciate it if you could spare a few moments to post a review on Amazon. It only need be a few words.

Thanks so much,

David Canford

ABOUT THE AUTHOR

Writing historical fiction, David Canford is able to combine his love of history and travel in novels that take readers on a rollercoaster journey through time and place with characters who face struggle and hardship but where resilience, love and forgiveness can overcome hatred and oppression.

He has also written two novels about the future, and a travelogue.

David has three grown up daughters and lives on the south coast of England with his wife and their dog.

You can contact him via his Facebook page or at David.Canford@hotmail.com

Printed in Great Britain
by Amazon